ONCE WAS
LOST

ONCE WAS
LOST

SARA ZARR

Little, Brown and Company
New York   Boston

Little, Brown and Company

Hachette Book Group
237 Park Avenue, New York, NY 10017
Visit our website at www.lb-teens.com

Little, Brown and Company is a division of Hachette Book Group, Inc.
The Little, Brown name and logo are trademarks of Hachette Book Group, Inc.

First Paperback Edition: January 2011
First published in hardcover in October 2009 by Little, Brown and Company

Library of Congress Cataloging-in-Publication Data

Zarr, Sara.
Once was lost : a novel / by Sara Zarr. — 1st ed.   p. cm.
Summary: As the tragedy of a missing girl unfolds in her small town, fifteen-year-old Samara,
who feels emotionally abandoned by her parents, begins to question her faith.
ISBN 978-0-316-03604-7 (hc) / ISBN 978-0-316-03603-0 (pb)
[1. Faith—Fiction.   2. Self-perception—Fiction.   3. Parent and child—Fiction.   4. Missing
children—Fiction.]   I. Title.
PZ7.Z26715On 2009   [Fic] —dc22   2009025187

10 9 8 7 6 5 4 3 2 1

RRD-C

Printed in the United States of America

Trouble is I'm so exhausted

The plot, you see, I think I've lost it

I need the grace to find what can't be found

Over the Rhine,

"Long Lost Brother"

Day 1

Saturday, early August.

The whole world is wilting.

Shriveling. Giving up. Dying.

Maybe not the *whole* world. Somewhere, I guess, it's not ninety-one degrees at four in the morning. I would like to be in that place. I would like to be somewhere, anywhere, that life feels possible and not smothered under a layer of heat and hopelessness. I'm tired of waking up every two hours in a puddle of sweat, and tired of every day discovering there's something else that's ruined or broken or falling apart. Yesterday it was the TV. Today, it's the ceiling fan in my room, the brokenness of which I discovered when I woke up wondering where the air went. I slipped out the sliding glass door into the backyard hoping for a miracle of something below eighty, and I now realize I can add the yard to the list of minor tragedies that make up my life these days.

The solar luminaries my dad put in last summer give just enough light that I can see the disaster it's become in this heat wave. Except I can't completely blame the heat. Honestly, it's looked like this for a long time. Dad's momentary burst of involvement via the luminaries and also painting the lawn furniture was just that — momentary. For about seventeen minutes last summer our family worked the way it's supposed to. The problems with the yard are just a symptom, really.

Everything out here reminds me of something. I can almost see the outline of my mom crouched at the base of the apple tree, mulching the roots, her blond hair held back with a blue bandanna; the curve of her neck, elegant. Even just a few months ago, when she was passing-out drunk, she still had that elegance. Classy is the word for my mother.

The clothesline strung up between a fence post and the metal eyebolt my dad screwed into the tree makes me think of the way he looked at her, laughing, when he said, "I can just imagine your undies flapping in the breeze on this thing, for all of Pineview to see. Your bra size will end up in the church newsletter if you're not careful."

"That would be funny if it weren't true," my mom said, but she smiled, too, and I know she liked it, Dad teasing her that way.

"Dad," I said, acting embarrassed. "Please." But I liked it, too.

That summer it wasn't too hot, and when the heat did climb there was iced tea on the back porch, my parents playing cribbage together after the sun went down, the game board balanced on my mom's tan thighs and my dad laying cards down on the arm of the chaise.

None of that lasted long. Probably all my good memories of the last year add up to three days.

I walk through the yard, making a mental checklist of what needs fixing. The two butterfly bushes have grown into each other and taken over the spot where my mom once had an herb garden, back when she still cared about things like cooking. The Mexican sage has completely run amok. The hollyhock plant that looked okay a few weeks ago has fallen over from its own weight, and lies across the flagstone path like a corpse. I step over to it, sweat trickling down the inside of my tank top and to the waistband of my pajama shorts. I try to get the hollyhock to stand up and stay up, but it flops back down over my bare feet.

I'm glad my mother isn't around to see this.

Instead, she's got the residents' garden of New Beginnings Recovery Center, neatly xeriscaped with drought-resistant plants that never ask for more than you can give them. Her room is neat. The cafeteria is neat. The visiting area is neat. She's been lifted, as if by the hand of God but in truth by the long arm of the law, out of this messy life.

I could make this yard look like the one at New Beginnings. All it would take are some supplies and time and maybe a book from the library telling me how to do it. Then, when she comes home, she won't have to see the same dead and dying things that were here when she left.

Ralph is hunkered down in the kitchen sink when I come in, cool porcelain all around him, and meows at me as if there's something I can do about the heat. I'd sit in the sink, too, if I fit. I lift him out and put him on the floor where he paces and meows and rubs his gray fur against my legs.

There's no cat food. There's barely any people food. I tear a few pieces off a leftover rotisserie chicken in the back of the fridge and toss them on the floor for Ralph, then pull an envelope from the stack of mail on the counter and start a grocery list on the back of it.

Soon I hear Dad up and moving around, and within a few minutes he appears under the archway to our open kitchen. I lift my head and he's rumpled and sweaty, his thick hair sticking up every which way, and staring at me like he's thinking of how to form the words that will make whatever it is not sound so bad.

"What," I say. It's not a question, because I know it's something. Every day it's something.

"Bad news."

I wait for it, thinking of some of the information that has recently followed that statement.

Grandpa's surgery didn't go like we'd hoped.

We're not sure if we can pay the tuition at Amberton Heights Academy next year.

Your mother's been in an accident.

"The air conditioner is on the blink," Dad says.

Of course.

He reaches down to scratch Ralph's head. "At least, I can't get it cranking. On the up side, the TV seems back in commission. I'm not sure how, but we're getting a picture again."

"My ceiling fan isn't working, either."

"You're kidding."

"No. And we need to buy groceries today." I hold up the envelope I've been writing on. "I'm making a list."

He comes close, smelling like someone who lives in a house where there is no air, and takes the envelope, turning it over to look at the front. It's a bill of some sort. "When did this come?" He rips into it.

"I don't know. The mail has been sitting here . . ." For a while. "Don't mess up my list."

He pulls out the bill, looks at it for half a second, and stuffs it back into the envelope. "I guess I should go through all of this," he says, looking at the pile.

"Yeah." There are a lot of things around here I can take care of, a lot of things I have been taking care of for a long time, but being fifteen and unemployed, money isn't one of them.

Dad searches through a pile of paper on the other end of the

4

counter. "Doesn't your mom keep coupons around here some-where?"

"Mom hasn't clipped coupons in at least three years," I say. I know, because it was my job to sit at the counter with the Sunday paper while Dad was at church getting ready for the service. I'd scan the coupons and deals, while Mom had her weekly anxiety attack about what to wear, and what to make me wear. She hated Sundays. Eventually I realized she wasn't even using the coupons, and I figured I'd be of more use helping Mom get dressed and ready and calm. "You look perfect," I'd assure her. And she always did.

Dad, of course, was never here for any of that, so he has no idea. He stops rummaging through the papers and looks at me. "Well, what is all this, then?"

It's stuff from the last four months that she was scared to throw away: old phone messages, flyers for events she was afraid she'd forget about, bank deposit slips. She used to like a neat house, everything in order, so the fact that she let that stuff pile up should have told Dad something. Obviously, he'd barely noticed the kitchen counter until right this moment.

"It's Mom's," I say. "Just leave it." I don't want her coming home from rehab and feeling like we went through the house, erasing her. "Can we stop at the hardware store when we go out?" I ask. "I want to get some stuff for the yard."

"Maybe I can find the part for your ceiling fan and get that working." He stares at me in that meaningful, fatherly way I can't bear anymore so I have no choice but to turn away and pretend to look in the fridge. "What else do you have going on today?" he asks.

"Nothing." I move an almost-empty carton of milk two inches to the right and close the door. "Unless you want to start our driving lessons?"

He shakes his head. "I can't today. I think you should make a plan. I think you should call Vanessa, or Daniel. Get out of the house. Go see a movie in an air-conditioned theater."

"Maybe."

"Sammy, it's not a suggestion. Okay?"

I nod. We've discussed this. Me being home alone too much, a habit I developed when I started to get afraid to leave Mom by herself. But she's not here now, so.

"I'm going to hop in the shower," he says.

I nod again, and watch him walk away, through the airless living room and down the hall.

Main Street in Pineview has exactly six not-so-creatively-named businesses:

Petey's Ice Cream

The Casa Nova Mexican Diner (only open three days a week)

Main Street Coffee

Main Street Gas & Garage

Main Street Bar & Grill (the "grill" part closed down years ago)

Main Street Hardware

We're two hours south of Medford, six hours north of Sacramento, and a day west of Denver, which puts us exactly . . . nowhere. We have parades on Memorial Day, Fourth of July, and Christmas. The Ten Commandments are still inscribed on a monument outside City Hall even after three lawsuits. Once a year people from all over the West come here for the Migratory Bird Festival. There's one public school for all grades, one private school (where I go, or *went*, I guess), one post office that's really a trailer off the pass, one library, and one grocery store where the whole town shops except for those who drive thirty-eight miles to the new Dillon's Bluff Wal-Mart. And seven churches, including Pineview Community, where my dad is the pastor.

Everyone knows him. Everyone *thinks* they know us, me. Everyone is wrong.

Even as we drive through town now, people in other cars and kids playing near the road recognize us and wave. Probably a third of the town's population helps pay the lease on our Taurus and the mortgage on our house, which gives them the right to say things to my dad like, "I see you got new tires there, Charlie. Are you sure the steel-belted are really worth it? They can't be cheap . . ." or "The front lawn at the house is looking a little ragged — do you need to borrow a mower?" Whenever I get new clothes I can almost see some of the women at church calculating how much we spent.

Everyone knows exactly how much my dad makes, and they think it's enough. Some think it's too much.

One time I was out with Mom when we ran into a congregant who owns his own tech company and gives a lot of money to the church. Mom was holding on to her cell phone, which she'd just upgraded to one of those that does everything so that I could have her old one, and this guy, this congregant, made a comment about it. "I guess you can keep your grocery list on that thing, if nothing else," he said. His big, jokey smile didn't hide what he was really saying: Why does a housewife need a fancy phone, especially when the church basically pays the cell bill, and shouldn't we use that money for new pew Bibles or an ad in the county yellow pages?

"Yes," Mom said, smiling back, drawing a perfectly but modestly home-manicured finger through a piece of hair that had fallen across her face. "It does wonders with grocery lists." But when the guy was gone, Mom said to me, "I guess we're not supposed to live in the twenty-first century," and tucked the phone into her purse, out of sight.

There's a lot of stuff like that we deal with. Those are just examples.

Now Dad pulls the car right in front of Main Street Hardware, and as he turns off the engine there's a little rattle coming from under the hood. I look at him. He's pretending not to hear it. After Mom's accident, and everything else, the last thing we need is car trouble.

The bells on the door of the hardware store jingle as we go in. A wave of air-conditioned air feels too cold at first, raising goose bumps on my arms, but then it's like heaven.

"Charlie, hey." Cal Stewart, who owns and single-handedly runs the hardware store, greets us. Or I should say he greets my dad and nods politely at me. "What can I do for you?" I like Cal, even though he never remembers my name. He's got woolly dark hair that's just starting to go a little gray, and wire-rim glasses that make him look smarter than most people in Pineview, and he's a lot nicer than the old couple he bought the store from a few years ago.

Dad and Cal discuss the ceiling fan issue, and I take advantage of the chance to walk the aisles of the store, running my hand over the different-size chains that hang from spools, looking into bins of glittering loose nails in every size, examining a dozen kinds of spackles and glues. There's something to make or fix or connect everything.

When he's done talking to my dad, Cal walks by the other end of the aisle and catches sight of me.

"Can I help you find something?"

"I'm thinking about doing something different in our backyard."

"Let's go to the outdoor section. Near the front."

My dad is up front, too, talking on his cell, something about the music for tomorrow's service.

Cal asks me, "So you want to do something different. Different how?"

"It's so hot," I say. "Everything's kind of . . . dying."

He leads me to a spinning wire rack of thin gardening books, many of them dusty and with pages that are starting to yellow from the sun. "Here's one on desert gardening. Technically, Pineview is high desert and not true desert, but it's got a lot of info on plants that don't need much water."

"Xeriscaping."

"Right." He hands me the book. "Is this for 4-H?"

"No," I say, surprised that he remembers. "Just for my house."

The last time I came here was to get wooden dowels. I dropped out of 4-H before I finished that project, which was supposed to be me and Vanessa teaching crafts at the Dillon's Bluff Senior Center, but my mom wasn't doing so well the day she'd promised to drive us to do the setup, and my dad was busy with church, and instead of telling the truth I told Vanessa that I'd given my mom the wrong date and Vanessa got mad and I dropped out rather than let her down again. Anyway.

"You'll probably need some of this," Cal says, leading me through the store to a pile of black plastic sheeting.

"What for?"

"To smother those water-greedy plants you're trying to replace." He hands me a bulky, folded armload of it.

"Ready, Sam?" my dad asks, eyeing what I've got and, I'm sure, calculating the price.

I nod. Cal rings us up and Dad pays with a credit card. We both exhale and try not to look too surprised when it goes through.

• • •

In the grocery store, Dad doesn't approve of my list. "Your mother lets you eat like this?" He puts a bag of chocolate-covered pretzels back on the shelf.

I stare at him.

"What?"

"Nothing." Just that you sound like a weekend dad who's been divorced for years, I think, not someone who allegedly lives in the same house as me.

He pushes the cart down the cereal aisle and throws in a box of cornflakes, the store brand that's always on sale and is not so much cornflakes as corn dust. To stop myself from complaining I turn on my heel and go off to the pet supplies, where I run right into Vanessa and her mom struggling with a twenty-pound bag of dog food.

"Sam!" Vanessa drops her end of the bag to the floor and hugs me.

It's only been a little over a week since I've seen her, but she looks like a whole different person to me. True, she's gotten her hair cut, and maybe she's a little bit more tan, but I mean she feels like a stranger — her voice, her soft arms around my neck, like it's been ten years, not ten days. I pull back, and wonder if she thinks I feel like a stranger, too.

"Didn't you get my messages?" she asks.

"I —" Whatever I say won't be true. How do you admit to avoiding your best friend?

Mrs. Hathaway, still grasping her corner of the dog food bag, saves me. "We wanted to invite you over for dinner sometime this week, if that would be okay with your dad."

She knows about my mom being gone, that's obvious, because normally she would have said, *if that would be okay with your mom.* Which makes me wonder how many other people from church know and when Dad is going to officially announce it so that I can stop playing the "I don't know if you know" game every time I run into church people, which is pretty much every time I leave the house.

"Yeah," Vanessa says, bouncing a little bit on the balls of her feet, "you can spend the night."

"I'll make your favorite Chinese chicken salad," Mrs. Hathaway coaxes. She always makes me feel like one of the family, as if she and my mom are still best friends and we all practically live at each other's houses, even though that hasn't been true for years.

"Come on, Sam." Vanessa is practically begging. I could make both my dad and Vanessa happy by simply letting the word *yes* come out of my mouth.

But I don't want to.

I don't want to be with people. I don't want to talk to people. I don't want to answer questions or pretend to be interested in conversations or activities.

"I'm really tired," I say. Which is true.

Vanessa's shoulders slump. "So?"

"Maybe. I'll call you." It's the best I can do. "I have to go find my dad." I pile a dozen cans of cat food into my arms.

"Okay, sweetie," Mrs. Hathaway says. "You let us know. Or just show up. You know our home is your home."

The way she says that, so sincere and warm and nurturing, makes me start to tear up unexpectedly, and I turn as I say, "Thanks," before she can hug me and make it worse.

"Call me, Sam," Vanessa says. "I miss you!"

"Me, too," I say automatically.

I find Dad in the produce section, loading the cart with vegetables. "There you are," he says. "Grab anything else you need and then we have to scoot. I haven't even started prepping tomorrow's sermon."

"Dad," I say, staring into the cart.

"What now?"

"It's all . . . ingredients."

He stops in the middle of filling up a plastic bag with broccoli and gives me a questioning look.

"Who's going to cook this stuff?" I ask.

"I thought . . ." Now he stares into the cart.

"It's not like *I* know what to do with it. She never let me in the kitchen when she cooked," I say. Cooking was the one thing she and I didn't do together. Everything else — shopping, cleaning, watching TV or movies, looking at magazines, gardening, polishing our toenails, doing our hair, trying on clothes, going for walks or runs — was the two of us. But when she was in the kitchen, even I was banished. It was the one place in her life where she was totally in charge.

"Haven't you noticed," I continue, "that your meals have come out of a can or the microwave since, like, Christmas?"

I take the bunch of broccoli out of his hand and put it back, along with the mushrooms, the little red potatoes, the baby squash. I keep the bagged salad and apples. Then I wheel the cart to the meat case and put back the package of ground beef and the whole chicken in favor of some pre-seasoned, pre-cooked chicken breasts.

"I could cook," Dad says weakly, but he knows I'm right. We're not the kind of family anymore that sits around the table to a balanced and nutritious meal to talk about our days. We're the kind that lives on stuff only requiring a person to work the microwave or add boiling water.

After filling our cart with stuff that meets these criteria, I pull Dad along to the checkout line. He's still in a daze, like he's only just now living in reality. I think of a line he uses in sermons sometimes: "Denial ain't just a river in Egypt." Funny how talking about things safely from behind a podium in church is different from really getting them in real life.

The cashier, a squat fifty-something woman who's worked here as long as I can remember, smiles big at us. Well, at Dad. "Hey, Pastor Charlie. Haven't seen you here in ages!"

And instantly he turns on his Pastor Charlie charm, going from sad and dazed to warm and present, like our grocery cart tragedy never happened. "Come to church and you can see me every week," he says with a grin. "You haven't been since your niece's baptism, am I right?"

I turn away, look at the candy shelf, and add some four-for-a-dollar chocolate bars to the conveyer belt. Meanwhile, the cashier and my dad are laughing it up. "Maybe I was hiding in the balcony."

"And maybe you weren't."

She loves it. Because all women love my dad. He's handsome enough even with the little soda-belly he's grown in the last couple of years, has all his hair, is youngish, charming, kind, a good listener, reliable, attentive, there when you need him. Those last four only apply if you aren't in his immediate family. Most of all he's the kind of man who would never cheat, and — as my mom pointed out to me once after a few drinks — that's exactly the kind of man women want to cheat with. "Ironic, isn't it?" my mom said, kind of laughing and kind of not. And I wanted to tell her how that isn't the sort of thing I want to know about or think about my own father, and please could we change the subject, but I don't think she really realized it was me sitting there with her. I mean she knew it was me, but when she's drinking she kind of forgets I'm her daughter and she's my mom. So the definition of appropriate topics of conversation tends to . . . expand.

Dad pays for the groceries with a check, which will float a couple of days while he figures out how to get money into our account.

Back in the car, he's still in his confident pastoral mode. "I'm sorry," he says, buckling his seat belt. "The food thing —"

"It's okay," I say, cutting him off. I turn up the air-conditioning full blast and lift myself off the seat a little to keep from burning my thighs on the vinyl.

"We'll sit down and talk about this. We'll make a plan for how to make sure we're taking care of ourselves and each other while Mom's away."

He's been saying this for two weeks now, been referring to this mythical conversation we're allegedly going to have, in which everything will be ironed out and processed and prayed over and resolved, and yet we somehow never actually have it.

We pull out of the lot. The air blowing into the car finally begins to cool. "I just have to get through church tomorrow," he says, "then on Monday we'll figure it all out." He glances at me. "Okay?"

The only response I can give is "Okay." I know that church comes first, and I didn't expect us to actually get five minutes to talk, and I guess I should be grateful we got groceries and went to the hardware store.

When we're almost home, I say, "I ran into Vanessa in the store. I think I'm going to spend the night over there." Because suddenly the prospect of conversation with other people doesn't seem as hard as going into that house, our house, staying there with no AC while Dad holes up in his office getting ready for tomorrow.

He gives my knee a light and happy smack. "Good, Sam. Good. I'm glad. You need to have some fun."

At Vanessa's house, the air-conditioning works and the mail isn't piled up and we sit around the table, all of us together, looking out onto a backyard where everything is under control.

"After dinner, you two can go out and pick some tomatoes," Mrs. Hathaway says as we all pass her our shallow bowls, which she fills with mounds of Chinese chicken salad. "Sam, you can take some home. We've got a bumper crop out there."

"Does this have onions?" Robby, Vanessa's seven-year-old brother, scrutinizes his dish. He always inspects his food with a funny kind of thoroughness — C.S.I. Dinner Plate.

"No, honey," his mom says. "Just scallions."

"I *love* scallions," I say, trying to help, making my eyes big and excited. "They're my favorite. Plus they make you super strong."

He's skeptical. "What are scallions?"

"Green *onions*," Vanessa says. Mrs. Hathaway gives her a look.

After we're all served, Mr. Hathaway extends his hands — one to Robby, on his left, and one to me, on his right. I take it, and Vanessa takes mine, and Mrs. Hathaway takes hers, and then completes the circle by holding Robby's. The prayer over the food is on the long side, as Mr. Hathaway covers not only the food but also each one of us as well as world events. His hand is rougher and bigger than my dad's, calloused from playing the guitar, which he does almost every Sunday.

"Amen," he finally says, giving my hand a squeeze.

This is what a family is supposed to feel like.

"How's your mother doing?" Mrs. Hathaway asks, as if it isn't the hardest question in the world to ask and answer.

"Fine." I eat a bite of salad. It's good. Mrs. Hathaway got this recipe from my mom.

"I know it's hard right now, but it's good that she's getting help."

"Mom . . . ," Vanessa says, and glances at me apologetically.

Robby asks, "Why does Sam's mom need help?"

I start to say that she had a little run-in with a fence post, which is true, but Mrs. Hathaway answers first: "She's sick, Robby. It's a disease. It's —"

"Like cancer?"

"Well, not quite." She looks thoughtful. This is a Teachable Moment. "But you could say —"

"We don't really need to go into this right now, do we, Nance?" Mr. Hathaway looks at Robby. "Sam's mom doesn't have cancer, bud. She's going to be fine."

"Yeah," I say to Robby, who's staring at me with eyes that are the same blue as Vanessa's. "She's going to be fine."

Out in the yard the ripe tomatoes are almost jumping into our hands. It's dusk, and the hummingbird moths hover and swoop around the lavender bushes while Daisy, Vanessa's golden retriever, walks the perimeter of the yard over and over. The Hathaways' yard is smaller than ours — they live a little closer to the main part of town where the houses are packed in a little more tightly. But it's definitely a better yard. They have a drip irrigation system, with a trickle of water constantly seeping out, just under the soil, and neat rows of summer produce. I wonder if I could do that without any help.

"My mom is so dumb sometimes," Vanessa says, straightening up among the tomato plants.

"It's okay. It's just . . . I didn't know she knew. And that you know."

"Why didn't you tell me?"

I move to another plant, but most of the tomatoes on this one are still a little green. "I was going to. You haven't been back that long."

Vanessa, along with almost the entire youth group except for me, went on a mission trip to Mexico. A lot of kids had to raise the money, but Mom didn't want me to because of how my dad's job already involves asking for money. When you stand there every week and pray before the offering plate is passed, people get funny about it.

I change the subject. "I love your haircut. It makes you look older."

She reaches a hand to her neck. "Really? It feels so short. This one old lady in Mexico thought I was a boy. Ugh."

"No, it's cute. And with the highlights cut off it looks more cocoa-y." I find a dark red tomato and pluck it from the vine. "Maybe I should chop my hair off, too." Even though I've always had long hair, the same ashy blond as my mom's, maybe short hair like Vanessa's could help me feel less weighed down by . . . everything.

"I like your hair the way it is."

We pick for a while, just listening to the crickets, before she says, "I wish you could have been there, in Mexico. It wasn't the same without you."

"Thanks. I wish, too."

"Sam? Is your mom really going to be okay?"

I blink several times and bend low, pretending to be interested in the plants. "Yeah. It takes time." That's what they said in the family orientation. *It takes time, and patience, and perseverance.*

"Are *you* okay?"

She wants me to talk, as in really talk, about my feelings. And I know she'll try again when we're in our sleeping bags tonight, and in the morning when we're getting ready for church. And every time, I know I won't be able to.

"Mm-hmm." I hold up my bowl of tomatoes. "Do you think this is enough?"

The outline of her head in the dimming yard nods.

Day 2

Sunday

There's a poster in the youth group room that probably came from some youth group–supplies warehouse in Texas or Colorado that I imagine is filled with T-shirts and coffee cups and rubber bracelets with what are supposed to be inspiring messages for The Youth, as everyone who is not The Youth calls us at our church.

The poster — now kind of curling and dusty — shows a bunch of multicultural-looking teens in fashions from five years go, falling all over each other on comfy couches, big smiles on their fresh faces, surrounded by pillows. One of them holds a Bible and a notebook in his lap. On the bottom of the poster are big yellow capital letters:

COMMUNITY HAPPENS!

Don't forget the exclamation point. Everything for The Youth has exclamation points.

When I was in sixth grade, I'd come to the church on Saturdays to help my dad get ready for the next day's services. I'd collect all the pencils from where they were holstered in the pew racks, sharpen them, and put them back. I'd restock the offering envelopes and make sure every pew had the right number of Bibles and hymnals. One time, my dad sent me down to the youth room to look for a missing communion tray and I stared at that poster and pictured myself in it, smiling, knee-to-knee with the other youth group kids, who would be my best friends. My community. It would be like having a whole bunch of brothers and sisters, and we'd know everything about each other. Because, as we're reminded all the time at church, community happens through sharing. "Getting real." With God. And with each other. Telling each other about the not-so-pleasant things that may or may not be happening in our lives. In theory, community ensues.

I believed in the theory, and expected that once I hit high school my life would be filled with all this understanding and friendship and spiritual bonding, and my faith would come alive, just like the poster promised. It hasn't really happened that way.

Now I look around at our monocultural faces, which are sort of smiling, but not nearly as happily as the poster faces. Mine least of all. It's not that I wouldn't like to share. It's not like I want to feel like this, live forever in this mood of resistance and suspicion and doubt. But I've been feeling this way too long to remember how not to. How would they react if I really did share, the way we're supposed to, and said: My mom is in "court-suggested" rehab and my dad has no clue how to deal with it or even talk about it, and I think I might be depressed? What if I said that?

Maybe this morning my dad will finally say something, officially, to the congregation about Mom, and then everyone will know and I can exhale. Then tomorrow, he and I will sit down and have that talk he promised about how things are going to be, how we're going to deal with it. And next Sunday, I can share, and finally make them all understand what I've been going through, alone, all this time.

For now, I sit with my lips pressed together while Vanessa, still touching the back of her neck every ten seconds like she's looking for the hair that used to be there, shares. She shares about how on the Mexico mission trip she realized how lucky we all are to have indoor bathrooms and clean drinking water. And Nick Shaw shares his excitement about moving into the dorms in a couple of weeks and also his anxiety because he doesn't know if he'll like his roommate and also he'll miss Dorrie. That's Dorrie Clark, who lives up in Dillon's Bluff and goes to a different high school but has been Nick's girlfriend for ten months. Their success as a couple is a disappointment to nearly every girl who's ever met Nick, me included. Not that I know him that well or sit around daydreaming about him. It's just that Nick is the kind of guy every girl wishes would choose her. He's a rare combination of tall and athletic and cute, and also sincere. He asked me to dance at a wedding once, and I just thought that was really nice, like he'd seen me sitting there looking bored and danced with me out of the kindness of his heart. I don't know any other high school boys who would do that.

Then Allie shares that while in Mexico, she woke up early one morning and something told her to go outside, and she did, and saw the sunrise and even though all of the poverty and despair had her wondering if God really pays attention, the beauty of the red and purple sky seemed to tell her yes, God is there, and knows what he's doing. "I really felt it." Her pale eyes are damp. "It was like a personal message but at the same time something everyone in the world could see. At least, everyone in that village, on that morning. It was . . . I don't know. Hope."

I glance at Daniel to check his reaction. He and Vanessa are the only ones who really know me, and at least understand my family a little bit. Even they can't totally get it, though, because no one can know what it feels like to be the pastor's kid unless they are one. Daniel, who normally would roll his eyes at Allie's personal messages from God, is staring at her, really listening, and nodding a little bit. He almost looks like he wants to say something, then notices my glance and doesn't. Instead, he scoots lower into his chair and scratches at his round face.

Allie talks some more and I start to envy her Mexico experience. Right now I would love to have a personal message from God. I want to believe the way I used to, when my dad or mom or sometimes both of them would pray with me at night and I would picture God listening, kind-eyed and bearded. He was real to me, as real as my own parents. I don't know when God stopped being someone I saw as my true friend, and turned into something I'm mostly confused about. But if I can believe that Allie believes, maybe that would feel close enough. Like if I can latch on to some third- or fourth-hand experience of real faith it will almost be enough to make up for what I've lost.

Through all the sharing, Erin, our youth group leader, leans forward with her elbows on her freckled knees while asking follow-up questions and making noises like "mm" and "oh" the way she does every week. The other thing she does every week, eventually, is turn her gaze to me and ask, "What about you, Sam? What's going on?" I always have to be coaxed. Now that I know that life in youth group isn't like the poster, I'd rather be helping out in the little kids' Sunday school class where everything is simpler — just coloring in scenes from uncomplicated Bible stories, then moving on to juice and animal crackers.

This time, Erin says, "We missed you on the trip, Sam. How'd you keep busy?"

I'm not sure who all this "we" is, because no one else has mentioned or commented on the fact that I didn't go. No one else seems to notice me at all, generally. I mean, at youth group stuff they do, because they have to, because Erin is vigilant about making sure everyone feels included. But a few of them go to my school and actively look the other way when they see me there, and more than once I've caught them all talking about some party or outing they obviously all had together without inviting me. Because I'm the pastor's daughter, I guess. As if I'd take notes and run to my dad if one of them swore or talked about sex or sipped a beer. I wouldn't.

Maybe it's got nothing to do with being the pastor's kid. Maybe it's just me.

They're waiting. What did I do to keep busy.

"I'm redoing our backyard. To make it more drought-friendly."

"Oh, cool," Erin says.

Thankfully, no one else has to come up with a reaction because Gerald Ladew, the organist and choir director, comes in to warm up the youth choir, a few of the junior highers — who meet in a separate group — trailing behind him. "Come on," he says to the high school members of the choir: Vanessa and Daniel and Allie and Paul. The Franklin twins are in it, too, but they're not here today. I can read music and sing a little, but I hate standing there in front of people so I faked not being able to carry a tune when Gerald auditioned us all in spring.

He herds them toward the old upright piano, warped and water-stained, another "just give it to The Youth" treasure, like our ratty couches and the coffee table with the one leg shorter than the others. The youth room is the dumping ground for stuff too ruined to be in congregants' actual homes anymore. There's still a pile of musty World War II–era pup tents in the corner some ancient church member thought we could use on the mission trip. No one had the heart to tell him no.

"Pretend that this is in tune," Gerald says, plinking out some notes. "Where's my soloist? Anyone seen Jody?"

Jody Shaw, Nick's thirteen-year-old sister, treks in late, because now she's the one who gets to help with the little kids' Sunday school, like I used to. She drags her feet, complaining it's too hot up in the sanctuary to sing, let alone put on choir robes.

"Don't be a whiner." Nick, whose hair is exactly the same shade of reddish-brown as Jody's, gives her a playful little shove with his foot as she passes by the couches, where we're sitting opposite each other, the only ones not singing — other than Erin, who's writing something on the wall calendar.

I can tell he's only teasing, because like I said, Nick is actually truly nice. But Jody whirls around, furious, and kicks out one skinny leg. Her foot makes contact with Nick's shin.

"Hey," he says, laughing. "Was that supposed to hurt?"

Jody's mouth makes a funny shape, and it's obvious she's about to cry. "It's okay," I say quickly. I hate knowing that someone else feels bad. "He's just kidding. And it is really hot. Don't wear robes," I say. "My dad won't care."

Jody nods and regains her composure. "I know." She looks at Nick. "Just be nice to me."

"I am. I will. Sorry, Jo-Jo."

I've never heard Nick call her that. It's sweet.

"Don't upset my soloist," Gerald calls, frowning in Nick's direction and running a hand over his balding, sweaty head.

"Okay, okay." Erin comes over and steers Jody by the shoulders to the piano. "It's the heat. It's making everyone crazy."

I study Nick's face while he watches Jody and the rest of them do their vocal warm-ups. I'm always watching Nick and Jody, and Kaleb and Kacey Franklin, and Vanessa and Robby. I can't imagine anything in the world better than having a sibling. Even if you fought sometimes, it would be worth it to always have that one person who knows what it's like to be part of your particular family. Someone you can look at to see who you are. And if I had a brother or sister, I wouldn't be the only pastor's kid.

Specifically, I always wanted a little brother, like Vanessa has. She and I were around eight when Robby was born and for like a year after that I kept asking my mom for a brother, too. That never happened. As far as I know, my parents didn't even try. I guess one was enough. Or too much.

Nick reaches to rub his shin and catches me staring. "It does kind of hurt," he says, sheepish. "Don't let Jody make you think I'm not nice to her. It's her. Ever since she turned thirteen it's like the sister I knew has been taken over by an alien. A very emotional alien." Then he smiles.

It's hard to explain how it feels when Nick Shaw smiles at you. Not butterflies or blushing. It just feels good. "I won't," I say. "Anyway, it's common knowledge that thirteen kind of sucks."

We hear the pre-service music starting upstairs.

Erin comes over and gathers her stuff. "That's our cue." Then she turns around and gives us a goofy grin. "And remember, this is the day the Lord has made." She holds out her hand, palm up, as if to say, "Well?" It's one of our little youth group rituals that's corny and embarrassing, but Erin always makes us, no matter what.

Nick and I complete the quote together: "Let us rejoice and be glad in it."

Nick pumps a fist on "glad" and Erin laughs, but while she does she looks at me with an expression I can only describe as worried.

I try to finish with an exclamation point.

The day the Lord has made is stinking hot. Throughout the service, people fan themselves with bulletins and offering envelopes and I can tell my dad cuts the sermon short so that everyone can go home and get on with life. Jody's solo was beautiful, though, her pure, sweet voice floating out of the choir loft and almost visibly rising in the warm air. But I couldn't focus on what she was singing, or on the rest of the music, or on the Old Testament reading, and I can't do it now as my dad is wrapping up the sermon. Because I'm waiting, waiting for him to say it.

After three Sundays with her gone, people have to be wondering what happened to my mom, and making up their own stories about it. Dad must know that the gossip could wind up worse than the truth if he doesn't tell them. And for a moment his mouth opens and his shoulders tense up and I know he's about to confess. That we're not perfect, that he's not perfect, that our family has problems, too, and we've covered it up for too long and that's not right when the church is supposed to be your second family.

The moment passes and he's lifting his hands to give the benediction.

I stand with him by the open main doors, in the path of a hot breeze and the blinding white of noon sun. Normally my mother would be standing here with us for this part of the Sunday ritual, when the visitors and regular attenders shake my dad's hand, hug him, tell him they liked the sermon, tell me I'm getting so tall, tell me I'm getting too thin, ask me what grade I'm in, and, now and most of all, ask us where Mom is.

"Oh, she's just been under the weather," Dad says over and over. "I'll tell her you said hello." He manages warm smiles when he says this, his straight teeth assuring everyone that everything is a-okay with the Taylor family. Nothing to see here, move along and God bless.

I can't stand to hear him anymore, so I step out of the glare of the sun and look into the sanctuary, where the light is coming through the small stained glass windows along the side that show different scenes from the life of Jesus. I can see the one of him turning water into wine, and half of the one of his baptism — just the corner of his shoulder with the dove about to alight. My favorite is out of view but I know it by heart: Jesus in a white robe standing next to a squinty-eyed Lazarus, who's fresh from the tomb after being dead for a few days. *Dead* dead. As a doornail. If you believe the story. Mary and Martha, his sisters, stand nearby, watching the whole thing, their arms held out in a kind of scared joy at the sight of their resurrected brother, like they're not sure if they should hug him or run.

I used to be able to picture myself there. Not just there with Lazarus but there for all of the miracles. There at the water/wine wedding. There at the baptism. On the hillside when he stretched a small lunch into a meal for five thousand. Growing up with those stories all around you all the time, you sort of buy in. You can't help yourself.

Now I think miracles are things that happen in stained glass, and on dusty Jerusalem roads thousands of years ago. Not here, not to us. Not when we need them.

In the car Dad pulls off his tie and strips down to his soaked undershirt. A half mile down the road, he says, "I know you're mad."

"You were going to tell."

"The timing didn't feel right."

I don't want to argue with him. All I want is to get home and eat something and have a cold drink and watch TV. If it works. I turn on the radio and find my favorite country station. "Did you fix my ceiling fan yet?"

"No. Sam . . ."

"It's okay."

"I'm sorry." He takes my hand, stilling my fingers. "And I don't mean about the ceiling fan."

For a second, I'm tempted to turn my hand over and let our palms meet, a small act of acknowledgment. Instead, I free it and hold it in front of the dashboard vent.

When I realize where the car is headed, I look at him. "Dad. Seriously?"

"It's the first Sunday of the month."

First Sundays mean brunch at the Lodge. Sometimes with Vanessa's family, sometimes with other people from church, sometimes just us. Once in a while we go even if it isn't the first Sunday. Exactly one month ago we went with Mom. She ordered a Bloody Mary, and then another, and then one more. Three drinks do not make Mom drunk. Three drinks keep her functioning, but Dad put his foot down about her drinking before church and maybe someone catching a whiff, so usually by the time church is done she's not doing so great. The servers at the Lodge know when they bring my mom a Bloody Mary to put it in a regular glass without a giant stalk of celery sticking out, and for all anyone knows she just really likes tomato juice.

"We're going to join Daniel's family today," Dad continues. "They invited us and I thought you'd enjoy that."

If I'm going to have to talk to anyone, it might as well be the Mackenzies, even if Daniel's dad can be a little bit loud. At least I know there won't be any lulls in the conversation. And I haven't spent much time with Daniel all summer, since he's been busy with summer school and I've been busy not spending much time with anyone.

The Lodge is this log-cabin-ish building on the edge of town, off a two-lane state road and up a winding dirt drive. It's kind of nestled up against the foothills and is the only place around here to go if you're having a special occasion: birthday, anniversary, graduation, stuff like that. It's also the only place open on Sundays, so people from all seven churches crowd into both floors of the restaurant and spill out onto the deck, which has plenty of shade and is rigged up with misters all around to keep it cool. That's where Daniel and his parents are sitting when we get there — at a table near the north corner of the deck. They wave us over.

As we walk to their table, people greet us. Well, they greet my dad. "Pastor Charlie," they call out, "enjoyed the sermon!" "Pastor Charlie! The new landscaping at the church building looks terrific!" "Pastor Charlie, are you here to poach my congregants again?" That last one comes from Pastor Egan of the Methodist church, and he says that every single time we see him. Every time. He's about seventy years old, and that's probably average for the other churches here. Pineview is the kind of town pastors come to when they want to retire but also want to still feel useful and make a little money. They pack up their empty nests (meaning: no other pastor's kids like me) and bring them here, so they can lead a rural church into its final years. That's what makes my dad and our church different — he's young, and the average age of our church membership is a lot lower than the other churches', and ours is the only congregation that's growing instead of dying. So Dad is Mr. Popular here at the Lodge, and he always turns on the charm.

"That's right, Bill," Dad says now to Pastor Egan, clapping him on the shoulders. "Bringing in the sheaves. That's why they pay me the big bucks."

Har har har.

I take the seat next to Daniel and say hi to his parents while Dad makes the final rounds of the deck.

"Samantha," Mr. Mackenzie says, taking a gulp from his coffee mug. He's already red and sweaty, even with the misters. "How's every little thing?"

My name isn't Samantha, but I've corrected him so many times it's getting embarrassing. "Fine."

Eventually, Dad makes it to our table and we order. I can tell Daniel's mom wants to ask about my mom: where is she, how is she, when will they be seeing her again. She doesn't, though. That's how you can tell people know something they aren't sure they're supposed to know, and how they know something is wrong. If they really had no clue about Mom's problems, they'd ask. Also, they would look at me, which Daniel's mother doesn't do.

"Danny Boy," Mr. Mackenzie says after we order, "tell Sam and Pastor Charlie all about your experience in Mexico."

"Sam's already been forced to sit through all that in youth group," Daniel says.

I look at him. "You didn't really say anything."

"He didn't? Tell Pastor Charlie," his mom urges. "Tell him . . . you know . . . what happened."

"Mom. It's kind of personal."

I keep staring at him. What could be so personal he won't say it in front of *me*?

His dad laughs and reaches across the table to grab Daniel's forearm and give it a jiggle. "It's Pastor Charlie. If you can't tell him, who can you tell?"

Dad smiles and says in his I'm-a-hip-grown-up-not-like-the-others voice, "You don't have to tell me, Dan. Or, we can talk about it later."

Daniel picks up his glass of water. There are giant sweat spots under his armpits. I try to think of a way to rescue him from this conversation, whatever it's about, but I don't try that hard because I'm just glad we're not talking about us.

"It's no big deal," Daniel says, "it's just —"

"No big deal?" his mom says softly.

Now I really want to know. "What?"

Daniel opens his mouth to speak but his dad interrupts. "Danny got a call while he was in Mexico," he says, looking at my dad, proud. "From the Lord."

"I'm thinking about maybe," Daniel glances at me, almost apologetic, "becoming a pastor. Maybe."

"Oh." I can't believe he didn't say anything to me.

"Hey," Dad says, "that's great."

"What's this 'maybe' business? You told us it was a calling, clear as day. There's no maybe in a calling." Mr. Mackenzie looks at my dad. "Right, Pastor Charlie?"

The food comes just as Dad is about to answer. Eggs and ham and hash browns for Daniel and his dad, pancakes for me, a poached egg on dry toast for Daniel's mom, who's always on a diet, and the French toast special for Dad. If Mom were here she'd get the two-egg breakfast with sausage, and toast with lots of butter. After a big greasy breakfast and three drinks and the relief of church being over, she'd be in her best mood of the week. Sometimes she'd get out a pen and start making lists on a stray piece of paper from her purse, or on the back of a church bulletin. Lists of things she planned to accomplish that week, like organize the garage or return phone calls. Lists of things that never actually got done.

I wonder if she were here now, what she'd say to Daniel's plans for following in my father's footsteps.

Dad positions his fork and knife over his food and then looks right at Daniel. I know he's about to make his pronouncement about Daniel's "calling." It's obvious that's why Daniel's parents invited us here in the first place. No matter what Daniel and his

31

family think God said to him about his future, it's what my dad says that really matters. You can see it in their eyes as they wait for him to speak.

"Working in church ministry is a great privilege. What is it they say about the military? It's the toughest job you'll ever love. When you sense God's calling, it might not be specific, like being a pastor." I can almost see Daniel's shoulders sag with relief, and I realize maybe the reason he didn't tell me is that he's already changed his mind. "Probably what you felt down in Mexico is the knowledge that your life has a purpose, and somewhere in that purpose you'll be serving God. Maybe as a pastor or missionary, but maybe not. You can serve God as a biologist or a literature professor or . . ." He glances at the guy refilling Mr. Mackenzie's coffee cup and smiles. ". . . as a waiter."

Mr. Mackenzie laughs. "Let's hope not!" And then Daniel laughs, and we all laugh, even the waiter. Dad's done it again. Said all the right things. Made everyone feel good. Spoken on God's behalf.

He blesses the food and I cut into my pancakes, staring at the foothills through the warm, misty air, wondering what God might be telling Dad about how we're going to fix our family. And if either one of them plans to finally relay that information to me.

When we get home, Dad tells me he's going to take a nap, like he does every Sunday after church stuff is over. Sometimes Mom naps, too, and so do I. We turn off the phone, turn off our cells, and escape into sleep. Right now, though, the last thing I feel like is lying alone in my quiet room with nothing to do but think. I plop down onto the living room sofa while Dad lurks in the hall like he wants to tell me something. As usual, the second we're alone, words don't come so easy for him.

"The ceiling fan in my room works," Dad says from behind me. "I don't mind taking the sofa if it's too hot out here for you."

I shake my head and pick the TV remote up off the table. Ralph yowls at me. I turn so that I can see my dad. "Did you remember to feed him this morning?"

Dad smacks his head. "Shoot. No. I'll do it right now."

"Never mind. I'll do it." I should have left him a note before I went to Vanessa's yesterday. "Go take your nap."

He follows me partway to the kitchen, then stops. "Okay. Come get me if you need anything."

He goes to his room and I collapse onto the sofa with the remote. The TV still works, for now. Cycling through the channels doesn't take long since we don't have cable. I can feel the last few weeks of summer stretching out in front of me, a hot expanse of days filled with . . . this. TV and Ralph. One of the things Dad and I need to talk about is whether or not I get to go back to Amberton Heights. Unless a pile of money falls from the sky in the next couple of days, I don't think so, especially now with Mom's expenses. And honestly, I don't care about school right now. Where I go, or even *if* I go. If I dropped off the face of the earth, that might be okay, too.

I put the remote down and lie back onto the sofa. I'm getting sleepy after all, pancakes heavy in my stomach. I doze off for a while, but then cheering on the TV wakes me. Golf. I cycle through the channels again and stay on a nature show, then fall back asleep. When I next wake up, it's nearly six, and I'm in a cramped position, sweaty. I sit up and move my neck back and forth to loosen it up, flipping through the channels again. While I'm doing that, I pass something that makes my heart skip, even before I really know what it is. I go back to it.

It's a screen-size picture of Jody Shaw.

I sit forward.

Jody, who just kicked Nick in the shin this morning. Jody, whose high, confident voice filled the church.

I put together the picture, the words on the screen, what the TV voice is saying.

Jody Shaw was taken off the street while walking to Petey's Ice Cream after church, wearing her favorite orange T-shirt. No one saw what happened. She was there one second, and gone the next. Gone.

Something rises in my throat — a sob that I'm scared to let out. This can't be happening. It can't.

I get up and move closer to the television. Mr. and Mrs. Shaw are on the screen now. And Nick. Mrs. Shaw crying and asking anyone who knows anything, anything, to call the police. Mr. Shaw says, "She needs us. And we need her."

Nick's face is blank, like someone has taken an eraser and rubbed out everything that was him.

The picture of Jody comes back up. She's in braids and braces and underneath her smiling face is Amber Alert information, phone numbers, website addresses. This is real. The rift in the world — the edge of which I've been teetering on for months — splits wide open, and I'm falling. "I know her," I say to the TV, then look around the room like there might be someone else to tell it to, but there's only Ralph, on the coffee table cleaning his paw.

"Dad?" My voice is too quiet to wake up someone sleeping in a room down the hall behind a closed door. I try to say it louder, because I don't want to move away from the TV. "Dad?" But it comes out even quieter than the first time. I back out of the room on unsteady legs, keeping my eyes on the TV as long as I can before I turn and stand outside my dad's room. "Dad." I push open the door. He's fast asleep, snoring lightly, the ceiling fan whirring above him. "Dad." A whisper now. I walk right up to the bed, where he's lying exactly on his half as if Mom is napping right beside him.

"Someone took Jody Shaw," I whisper. I lay one finger on his chest and prod him. "Daddy. Someone took Jody Shaw," I say again.

His eyes flutter open. "Sam? Are you okay?"

I can't think of the right answer to that question.

"Did you just say something about Jody Shaw?"

I nod, and swallow hard.

"She's gone."

Day 3

Monday

My alarm goes off at five fifteen.

I reach to turn it off, resting my hand on its white and orange feet — it's a plastic rooster with a clock in the belly. It's ugly and annoying and something for eight-year-olds. Dad gave it to me back then, back at age eight, when my mom forgot to wake me up on time and I missed the field trip to the dairy in Clarkville. That was unusual. The thing about Mom's drinking is that she's done it her whole adult life and ninety-five percent of the time it was never a *problem* problem. Then all of a sudden and not that long ago, it went to more like eighty-seven percent. Soon after that, it dipped down to maybe sixty-two. Back when I was in elementary school, my mom forgetting *any*thing was a rare event, especially anything having to do with me. She was always there for me way more reliably than my dad. If she hadn't been in the accident and gotten cited, she'd be here right now.

I pick up the clock and hold it to my chest for a minute before turning it over, taking the batteries out, and getting up to put it in my trash can. I don't know why I've kept it this long.

As I'm doing that, the news about Jody hits me all over again.

You know when you're having a nightmare that feels so real, and the moment you first begin to realize it's a dream comes and in those few seconds you feel like the world is in perfect order and you're safe? That all the stuff you thought was horribly wrong was only your imagination?

This is the opposite of that.

I sit on the edge of my bed, the air still and warm in my small room, and put my head in my hands. "God," I say. And try to follow it with a real prayer. Something that will bring Jody back. If I thought we needed a miracle before, now there's no question. I want to close my eyes and ask for what's right, and open them and have everything fixed. As I try to form the words, I only get angry. Why should I even have to ask? You don't have to be all-powerful and all-knowing to figure out that this is a tragedy in need of divine intervention. I lift my head without actually asking the questions I have: *How could you? Why would you?* I used to be able to pray like that — angry prayers, doubtful prayers. Mom always says that doubt is just another way of expressing faith, and sometimes I'd hear her mutter things to God, like, "Thanks a lot. I guess we'll chalk *that* one up to character development," or, "I eagerly await your explanation for this in the hereafter, assuming there is such a thing." Like her, no matter what I prayed, I just always took for granted someone was listening.

Now, I don't know. This is different than doubt. This is something I've never felt before, a total absence of whatever it is that's made me who I am, on the inside, all my life.

Last night, Dad went over to Jody's house to be with her family. He asked if I wanted to go with him. I couldn't.

"I'll just feel like I'm in the way," I said from the hallway, where I watched him get ready to leave.

"Are you sure?"

He was strangely calm-looking, his tan face smooth, his hair in place, jaw set. It dawned on me that in a way he's been prepping for a tragedy like this all his life; he's like an actor getting his ultimate role. For someone whose career is believing in God and convincing other people to, this is exactly the kind of thing that would give him a chance to really prove that everything he's been saying is true. I don't mean it like he's faking it. I just mean I looked at him last night and saw he was ready. Like everything else, even what's happened with Mom, has been practice.

I knew he'd go over to the Shaws and know what to say. And I knew I wouldn't.

"I'll stay here and answer the phone and stuff," I said, because everyone from church would be calling. "What should I tell people?"

With no hesitation, he said, "Tell them I'm with the Shaws, and I'll be sending out an e-mail blast tomorrow letting them know specific ways they can help — meals, money, et cetera. Meanwhile, they should watch the news and do whatever the authorities say."

I watched him put his cell phone and wallet in his pockets.

"But maybe Jody will come back home, and all that won't happen."

"Maybe," he said, not sounding very convinced. "Hopefully."

I followed him to the front door and said, "I should call Mom."

He turned, and for a second his calm confident look went away. "Yeah, good idea." He kissed my cheek. "Lock the door after me."

Not as many people called the house as I expected — I guess they were all watching the news, like I was. Not that there was any actual information since the very first report. In place of information, the local anchor, Melinda Ford, moderated filler. Statistics. Speculation. Interviews with experts who tried to come up with theories about who could have done it, experts telling parents how to keep their kids from feeling afraid, experts discussing past cases of missing children. Experts who seemed to know everything except where to find Jody.

Vanessa called my cell, crying. "It's so awful," she kept saying, through her sobs. "It's so awful."

I had no response except "I know."

Daniel called, too. "I bet she'll be back tonight. I bet she will. I bet it's just a mistake."

What kind of mistake? I wanted to ask. Like she went out for six hours and forgot to call home or leave a note? What could a thirteen-year-old even find to do for six hours in Pineview? But I figured he knew all that and was just saying out loud what he wanted to believe, so I said, "Yeah."

I called New Beginnings to talk to my mom but all I got was the voice mail system telling me to call back during operating hours, so I left a message. Residents aren't allowed to have their cell phones. I pictured her at breakfast in the morning in the New Beginnings cafeteria, everyone reacting to the news. And her sitting there, probably the only one who *really* knows the Shaws, the only one who has put her arms around Jody in a hug.

Mostly, I couldn't stop thinking about Nick.

Not having a brother or sister, I couldn't imagine how he'd feel. I thought about how he'd been with her at church that morning, teasing but sweet, calling her Jo-Jo. How much they looked alike. Also I kept going over and over that time he asked me to dance at that wedding at the church last spring. An old, slow song buzzed from the speakers that are too small for the huge fellowship hall and we danced and made small talk. At first I kept thinking things like: Why is he asking me to dance when he's already been with Dorrie for months? It's because I'm the pastor's kid. And/or maybe Vanessa went up to him and said something like, "Sam's been sitting alone all night. Go ask her to dance." I decided he simply did it because that's the kind of nice person he is. Worst case scenario, it was a pity dance, and for someone like me — who's never had a boyfriend, never been kissed, never even held hands — a pity dance is still appreciated. Being that close to another warm body was . . . I don't know. Perfect. I still remember exactly how it felt, Nick's hands light on my back, like I could break.

And something about that, even though it happened awhile ago and we're not what you'd call friends, still makes me feel close to him. Which makes me feel close to this, to what's happened to Jody. Closer than I'd feel if she weren't Nick's sister.

So I watched the news and thought about him, and then Melinda Ford said that anyone who wanted to help search should meet up at the library at six this morning. Within minutes, my phone rang. It was Erin, saying that she was calling the whole youth group. Anyone who wanted to search should meet her at the library in the morning and we'd do it, we'd look for Jody.

Which is why my alarm went off at five fifteen.

I dress, pull my hair into a ponytail, and slip on my hiking sandals, having random fantasies about being the one to find Jody. I picture myself with a big group of searchers, combing the foothills and calling Jody's name, wandering off a little, on my own. Catching a glimpse of something and going farther away to investigate. Finding her, crouched, alone and scared. She'll reach out her hand and I'll sit with her until she feels safe, then I'll lead her to the other searchers.

Like Jesus, coming back to the flock with his one lost lamb.

I go into the bathroom, digging under the sink for a tube of sunscreen, shaking my head at myself for even remotely thinking it could be like that, reminding myself that I don't even know anymore if I believe those Sunday school stories are true.

Dad's not in his room when I check to see if he's awake. I find him in his small, cluttered study at the end of the hall, staring into space, a cup of coffee on his desk.

"Did you sleep in here?" I didn't hear him come in last night.

He glances up, then looks at his watch. "I didn't sleep at all. Anywhere. How about you?"

"A little bit. How are the Shaws?"

Dad shakes his head but can't talk. The energetic confidence of last night has left him totally.

If I let it stay silent, he might start crying, so I tell him about how I called Mom and left a message, that I'll try again later. "We can both talk to her."

He shuffles some papers on his desk. "I'm not sure about today's schedule. I told Jody's folks I'd meet them at the search site this morning to be with them at the press conference."

"Well I won't call until we can both talk to her," I say. When he doesn't react I remind myself that he's under a lot of pressure, and that obviously Jody's family comes first right now. I change the subject. "Did you get my note?"

About the search. I left it on the fridge before I went to bed last night.

"Your note? Oh, yes."

"So can I go?"

"Absolutely. I think it's a great idea." Now he's sounding more like himself, like an athlete warming up for the day's race. He scratches his unshaven face. "I guess I should take a shower if I'm going to be on TV." He gets up, and when he passes me in the doorway, gives me a long look and a short hug. "Get yourself some breakfast. I'll be ready in ten minutes."

• • •

Downtown feels strange, unfamiliar, even though in most ways it looks like it always does on a summer morning. The farmers' market is set up across from the library, like always. Chickadees call to each other from the cottonwoods growing around the square. Even the record heat is almost normal. It's not like it's ever *cool* here in summer.

But you can sense there's been a shift in the universe, that from now on no one who lives here will walk down Main Street and feel the same as they did yesterday, before this happened. It's not just what looks wrong, like crowds of people milling around the library at six AM, news vans, a media tent. It's what feels wrong, what *is* wrong, and all of a sudden I don't want to move from where we're standing, on the curb kitty-cornered from the library, to the other side of the street. I want to be back home, asleep, not awake yet in the new reality.

"There's Erin," Dad says, pointing to the edge of the crowd that's gathered. She's with one of the Franklin twins — Kacey — and also Daniel. Vanessa texted me this morning to say she's coming, too, but I don't see her yet. "You'll be okay?" Dad asks.

"Yeah."

"Stay where people can see you."

"I know." For some reason I'm still not moving, lead in my legs and in my heart.

"I mean it, Sammy, don't go off alone."

"Dad, I know."

He takes a few steps, then looks back, waiting for me to get going. "You want me to walk you over there?"

If I could say exactly what I'm thinking, I'd turn to my dad and say, *Please, take me home.* I'd tell him about how I don't feel like me anymore.

43

Instead, I act like he's being overprotective, like I'm fine. "Nothing's going to happen to me between here and twenty yards from here." I make myself start across the street, and wave him toward the media tent. "The Shaws are probably waiting for you."

"Okay, honey. Call me when you're done."

By the time I get to Erin and Kacey and Daniel, there are tears in my eyes. Daniel opens his arms and I take the hug. His big stomach and familiar, fruity-smelling sweat are comforting. Then Kacey Franklin gives me a quick hug even though we aren't really friends. She's one of those people who always seems to be changing the subject when I walk into a room, and said at youth group one time that she only comes to church because her parents make her and she can't understand how anyone could really believe. I think she thinks we must be so different.

Erin, wearing hiking shorts, her hair held back by the sunglasses that rest on top of her head, puts her arm around me and squeezes tight. "Hey."

I spot Vanessa walking quickly from down the block.

"I guess this is all of us," Erin says, waving to Vanessa and checking her watch.

Vanessa doesn't say a word, just receives hugs from everyone and holds on to my hand. We all go over to the volunteer registration table where people are crowded, chattering about how awful this is, how unreal. Some people hold cardboard cups of coffee, and donuts, like it's social hour. There are a lot of people from church here, and a couple of the faculty from Amberton Heights Academy. Gerald Ladew, the organist and choir director, stands on the fringes of the crowd. I catch his eye and give him a sad wave; he looks away, his face pinched like he might cry. So many people are connected to Jody in some way. It's like a Venn diagram of tragedy.

We pick up orange mesh vests and bottles of water, and Erin talks to one of the coordinators. Then she explains it to us.

"They're sending people out in groups of three, mostly," she says. There are five of us. Vanessa squeezes my hand tighter. "But I told them we want to stay together. Okay?"

We all agree.

Then, one of the volunteer coordinators — Darlene, according to her name tag — comes over and tells us that we're going door to door. We've been assigned the neighborhood west of Main and we're asking the residents questions, passing out flyers, looking for anything unusual.

"What about searching?" I ask. "What about actually looking for Jody?"

"We really do need people going door to door." She touches my arm. "It's just as important."

It's not how I pictured it. I thought we'd be hiking through scrub forest and foothills. Instead, we cram into Erin's little car and drive closer to our assigned area, then walk the roads of Pineview in our orange vests, dividing up and sharing tasks. It turns out Kacey is pretty good with maps. A different side of her comes out as she looks at it and points with her pink-polished nails to show us where we are and where we're going. "We should start this way," she says, definite, and we follow her. Erin and Vanessa decide they'll knock on doors and ask questions while Daniel and I search the yards wherever anyone is home and says it's okay, keeping watch for anything strange.

It's still early; the streets are quiet. I've been inside some of these houses. I recognize one as the home of my third grade teacher, Mrs. Benchley, who always had an end-of-the-year party at her house for all the parents and kids. We'd have relay races and water balloon tosses on the big field behind her house. Now Mrs.

Benchley doesn't live there anymore, and Daniel and I are walking across that same field, eyes to the ground, searching for we don't know what.

I look to the instruction sheet Darlene gave me for help. "It says to call the victim's name," I tell Daniel when we stop at the next house. We have to look in garbage cans and recycling bins and in any corner or hidden spot where someone could conceal something or someone.

Erin and Vanessa talk to the resident on the porch; Kacey leans against a car in the driveway, waiting. The first time Daniel calls Jody's name, they all stare, alarmed. "It says to call her name," I repeat, this time to Erin and Vanessa, and Kacey, who looks away.

He does it at the next house, and it still sounds wrong. By the third stop we're getting used to it, but there's one moment after he says her name and I hear the thunk of a garbage can lid being dropped that I feel that sob rising up again, and I have to press my hand against my mouth to keep it in. We're looking for Jody — Nick's little sister, Mr. and Mrs. Shaw's daughter — in garbage cans.

"Well this is depressing," Daniel says as we all cross to the next block, if you can describe the layout of Pineview as blocks. It's really more like clusters of old farmhouses, with newer houses sprinkled in between, now that most of the farmland has been divided up into residential tracts.

Kacey makes a check mark on the map with a little golf pencil, and says, stopping at the corner, "We could either zigzag across streets to get both sides at once, or do a loop back to the car and get the other side of the street on our way back." She turns the map for a different view. "Or . . ."

"*God*, Kacey," Vanessa blurts, "how can you be so . . ."

Kacey sweeps her blond-streaked bangs to one side. Her eyes are steady. "So what?"

"So efficient."

"Okay," Erin says, putting one hand on each of their shoulders. Kacey pushes it off. Daniel's eyebrows go up.

"It's what I'm good at," Kacey says to Vanessa, defensive. "I'm good at maps and organization and checking things off lists." Her body relaxes a little. "It's the only way I know how to help, okay?"

They stare at each other until Erin says, "You're doing great, both of you."

"Sorry," Vanessa mutters.

"Zigzag, loop, do a figure eight, whatever," Daniel says. "Just tell us where to go, Kace."

So we proceed.

At a house on the next block, Daniel and I finish in the front and back yards but Vanessa and Erin are still talking to whoever lives there, and Kacey stands near them, taking notes. Daniel and I find a shady spot under a blue spruce and wait, drinking from the bottles of water we got at the library. I'm thinking about Jody but want to talk about something else, just to get relief from tragedy for two seconds.

"What was it like?" I ask him. "In Mexico. When you . . . got the call or whatever."

"Oh. Yeah, well, first of all I'm sorry I didn't tell you about that before."

"Did you hear a voice or something?"

"No. It's really hard to explain." He wipes his face with a corner of his T-shirt. "We were in the middle of nowhere, and it was so, I don't know, desolate. In this way that makes you have deep thoughts. I thought about how so much of the world needs help, and asked myself . . . what could I do?"

"You could be in the Peace Corps," I offer. "You could be a doctor. You could be a teacher. You could be a businessperson who donates money to good causes, Daniel, you could help people a lot of ways. I just don't understand why a *pastor*."

He gives me a funny look. "I guess when I say people need help I don't mean that kind of help."

I look down. I know he really likes my dad. And maybe my dad does help people in some intangible important way. It's just hard for me to see when he's never home.

"Anyway," Daniel says, "possibly I was just heat-struck and hopped up on too much Mexican chocolate and too little sleep. I shouldn't have told my dad. He told my grandpa, and now my grandpa e-mails me like every day with stuff he finds on the Internet about the best seminaries, and articles about quote-unquote trends in church management and lists of stuff to read. It's going to be this total disaster now if I don't do it."

"You're only fifteen."

"Yeah, well, so was Mary when God told her she was going to give birth to Jesus, according to your dad."

I finish my bottle of water. Vanessa, Erin, and Kacey are descending the front steps of the house. "My dad isn't right about everything."

An hour later we don't have one single piece of new information, and we're slowing way down in the heat. We get to a house where some little kids are playing in the front yard, running through the sprinkler. After going through our question and search routine, Erin asks the mom of the kids if we can take a rest on her porch, already lowering herself onto one of two Adirondack chairs. Kacey takes the other one. Vanessa stays standing while Daniel sits next to me on the wide steps after the mom goes down them to deal with a crying kid.

"I think I melted off ten pounds of blubber already," Daniel says. "By the end of the day I should fit into my skinny shorts."

Erin leans forward to touch her toes, stretching out her back. "How do you guys feel?"

"Hot," Daniel says. "But I can keep going for a while."

"Me, too." I'm not giving up on Jody just because of a little heat, but I wish I'd actually eaten a good breakfast the way my dad suggested, because I do feel a little bit weak.

"I'm fine," Vanessa says. Then she looks at Kacey. "You seem good."

"Yeah."

They all start pulling phones out of their pockets and checking for messages and sending texts, so I get mine out, too. No missed calls. No texts. Nothing from my mom.

One of the kids waves to me, grinning big. She's happy. She thinks she's living in the same world that she lived in yesterday. Her yellow tank top has a silver glitter sun on the front and her shorts pocket has Elmo and she's got sprinklers and a friend to play with.

A couple of weeks ago at church I passed by a Sunday school room where Jody was helping the kids with a craft project, sitting in one of the tiny preschooler chairs, her braids hanging dangerously close to the glue and glitter used to decorate pictures of Jonah in the belly of the whale. I stopped and watched, not because of Jody, but remembering my preschool self and how my mom would hang my Sunday school craft projects on the fridge. And what was on the fridge kind of summed up my faith. It was my parents', really, only belonging to me by default and habit.

Erin's feet appear on the step next to me. "Ready?" she asks.

But when I stand up, I wobble a little. "Whoa," says Erin, steadying me. "Are you okay?"

"Yeah, just lost my balance for a sec."

After another hour, Erin says, "We should break again. Or stop. The heat's getting to be a little much."

"Getting to be?" Daniel asks.

"No . . . ," Vanessa says.

I agree with her. "There are a lot of houses still. Let's eat, then keep going." I shield my eyes and look down the road. "Sykes is three blocks that way, right, Kacey?" I point in the direction of the little gas station and convenience store where my mom used to send me on my bike for ice or toilet paper emergencies. I notice that my hand is shaking. I lower it before the rest of them see.

I'd passed hungry a long time ago, and passed thirsty way before that. Now I'm hit by a sudden wave of dizziness.

"Are you sure that place is open for business?" Erin blots sweat off her forehead with the back of her arm. "It always looks so deserted."

Her words sound funny. Murky and slow.

"Yeah, I don't know," Kacey says. "Maybe we should head the other way, toward the QuickMart."

When was the last time I was at Sykes? I try to remember. My thoughts fuzz.

"As long as there's a bathroom."

Who said that? Probably Daniel. But it's hard to distinguish their voices. They're getting farther away, either because I've stopped moving or they've kept going, or both. All I know is that my legs don't feel altogether . . . there. As bright as the sun is, the houses and trees and lawns around me are going dim and grainy.

"Sam?" someone says. "Are you okay?"

I want to answer but my tongue suddenly feels swollen to the size of my mouth.

I'm sinking slowly onto a lawn. The grass against my cheek is at least a little bit cooler than the air. I want to stay here and rest my eyes, so I do.

"Sam? Sam, can you hear me?"

I try to nod, and am able to open my eyes for a second. Erin's nice face shimmers and fades. Daniel looks panicked.

"Don't tell my dad," I say, and close my eyes.

"Sam, stay with us."

"Bring the hose over." That's Kacey. She *is* very efficient.

"Okay, Sam." Erin's voice is close and soft. "Just hang in there." Hands touch me, lift my head.

Something cool runs over my neck. I open my eyes and look past Erin, past Daniel, through the leaves of a nearby tree and into the sky. I attempt to see past the sky, and into God's heaven, from where he watches, doing nothing.

Day 4

Tuesday

I wake up in the dark of my room, the edge of my sheet fluttering from the small fan someone has put on the floor nearby. My head throbs behind my left eye, pain spreading to my temple and around my jaw. I try sitting up. Dizziness forces me back down. That's when I see my father sitting in the desk chair he's pulled over to the bed.

"Hey," he says, putting a hand to my forehead. "How are you feeling, sweetheart?"

I don't know what time it is, how long I've been here. The blinds are drawn. I crane my neck to look at the rooster clock — ticking away as happily as ever — before remembering it's supposed to be in the trash. "Thirsty."

"Here." He picks up a glass from the nightstand and holds the straw to my lips — a bendy straw with red stripes, the kind my mom always gives me when I'm sick. "It's a mix of juice and water."

I sip, then let the straw pop back out of my mouth. "What happened?"

"You don't remember?"

"I remember looking for Jody."

I remember Daniel looking worried. I remember the way everything disappeared, a mirage in the heat. Hands cradling my head. That the time felt infinite and strange but when I opened my eyes they told me I was only out for a few seconds. "Can you stand up?" Erin had asked, with Vanessa crouched beside her, putting a hand on my shoulder. I did try standing but everything spun, and Erin and Daniel helped me up and took me into someone's house and the rest is blurry.

"You were dehydrated," Dad says now. "And overheated. And very weak. Did you even eat breakfast yesterday?"

"Yes."

"A good breakfast, or the usual junk?"

"The usual junk." It hurts my throat to talk.

He shakes his head and holds the glass while I take a few more sips. "Sam," he says, "I wish you'd eat a vegetable now and then."

I release the straw from my teeth. "For breakfast?"

"You know what I mean." He sets the glass down. "I rescued Rooster from the garbage can. He only needed a fresh battery. Good as new."

Instead of telling him I don't want the clock anymore, I say, "Thanks." With my eyes on the ceiling, because I can't stand to look at his face if it's bad news, I ask, "Did they find Jody?"

There's a long pause. I close my eyes for a few seconds then open them again.

"No," he says. "They didn't. Not yet. Searchers went out again today." He holds the straw to my lips again. "Drink."

I take another sip. Ralph trots into my room and jumps on the bed with a soft grunt. I run my fingers through his fur. "Did you talk to Mom?"

"I haven't had a chance to call."

"She didn't call us back?"

He shakes his head.

Then I hear noises from the kitchen — running water, dishes clinking. "Who's here?" I ask.

"Oh." He glances at the door. "Erin came by to check up on you, and now she's cleaning up a little. I couldn't stop her. She's going to hang out here with you while I'm out."

"Where are you going?"

"Over to the Shaws. And to the church office."

"I don't need Erin to stay with me." I try sitting up again, to prove that I can take care of myself. My head spins and I flop back down.

"Right," he says.

Ralph walks to the end of my bed, where he can feel the fan, and curls into a ball, head up, the tip of his tail twitching.

"How about something to eat?" Dad asks me. "What sounds good?"

"Nothing."

All I can think about is Mom not calling back. She knows my cell number backwards and forwards. If she were here, now, with all of this going on with Jody, we'd be inseparable. Maybe she didn't get my message. But even if she didn't, wouldn't she call me as soon as she heard the news about Jody? To see how I'm feeling, to make sure I'm okay? To talk and speculate and wonder?

"You have to have something," Dad says.

"Just bring me whatever."

"Sounds like something I can handle." He stands, kisses the top of my head.

But it's not Dad who ends up bringing me food, it's Erin. She comes in with a plastic tray she must have dug up from one of the bottom kitchen cabinets. Arranged on it are a turkey sandwich, a peach, and yet more of the water/juice combo I'm already getting sick of.

"Hey there, gorgeous," she says, setting the tray down on my desk. She holds up the peach. "This comes compliments of Vanessa, from the tree at her neighbor's house. She guarantees it's a perfect peach, just how you like it. She says to call her when you're up to it."

She hands it to me. I put my nose to the fuzzy skin. It does smell perfect, and for the first time I actually feel hungry. "Did my dad already leave?"

"He did."

Without saying good-bye.

Erin sits on the edge of my bed, folding her toned leg under her. "So that was exciting, yesterday, huh?"

"Sorry."

"What are you sorry for? The heat was crazy. You weren't the only one on the search who went down."

"Really?" I bite into the peach; it's soft but not mushy, the flesh pulling easily away from the pit. I wipe juice from my chin. "Did you guys keep going, after? Did you finish the map?"

"Not quite," she says, "but don't worry about that, okay?"

"Sorry," I say again.

"Stop apologizing, you," Erin says, giving my arm a fake punch.

I take a few more bites of the peach. I want to be alone, I want to call Mom, I want a tuna sandwich, not a turkey sandwich, and I want it the way my mom makes it. "You don't have to stay," I tell her. "I'm fine."

"Your dad made me promise not to let you convince me to leave." She gets the sandwich from my desk and hands it to me. "He also made me promise to make sure you eat." Apparently she takes this command very seriously, and literally; she sits there while I eat the whole thing and finish the juice.

I hand her the glass. "Happy?"

"You don't even know." She watches me for a little while, her feet propped on the edge of my bed while she sits in the chair. "It was actually kind of scary for a couple minutes there, yesterday. I imagined trying to explain to your dad that you collapsed on my watch."

"I'm fine."

"I know. But I'm saying that I care about you and don't want anything to happen." She nudges my hip with her foot. "Get it?"

I nod.

"And speaking of caring about you, you know if you want to talk to me about your mom or anything else, you can."

"Okay." I guess I knew she knew, that it would be something my dad would have told her, probably a long time ago. She waits, like I'm going to do it right now, just open up about what it's been like to be part of a family that everyone on the outside thinks is so perfect, to have a dad everyone loves but who isn't there for me, and then on top of that to lose my mom the particular way she's been lost.

When Erin finally gets that I'm not going to talk, she lifts her feet from the bed and stands. "You want to get up and walk around the house a little bit, test out your legs?"

"In a minute."

As soon as she leaves, I roll over in bed with my back to the door, and cry, and then go back to sleep.

Forty-eight hours since thirteen-year-old Jody Shaw disappeared from the quiet streets of Pineview, frustrated investigators and a shocked community are still without answers. While one witness account places a blue sedan near Jody's last known location, police cannot confirm. Authorities are following several leads in the case but no arrests have been made. More than three hundred volunteers turned out yesterday to help with the search; unfortunately, the record heat curtailed efforts and sent several volunteers to the hospital with heat exhaustion, and there's no sign of cooling in the forecast. The search resumed early this morning; we'll be updating you throughout the evening with any breaking information.

This is Melinda Ford, reporting live from Pineview, where at least one family is waiting to hear some good news.

Erin and I are on the sofa, watching the news. Melinda Ford stands on Main Street, her eager face powdered sweatless and her blond bob sprayed into total submission. One time Mom and I watched her report on an apartment fire in Dillon's Bluff, her colored contacts—enhanced eyes wide and alive, with the flames and smoke shooting up behind her.

"There's nothing that girl loves more than bad news," Mom said, before changing the channel with one hand, her wine glass in the other. Melinda Ford is always "that girl" to my mom. "Someone should introduce that girl to the concept of the roots touch-up." "One day that girl needs to learn the correct pronunciation of 'nuclear.'"

I start to say something like that to Erin, something my mom would have said, but it would feel a little bit like a betrayal to be dissing Melinda Ford without Mom there. And I miss her.

I don't miss coming home from school not sure about whether I'd find the functional or nonfunctional version of her.

I don't miss making up excuses when people from church would call to make sure Mom was okay after skipping a meeting of the building committee or failing to show up for a scheduled lunch.

I don't miss the way Dad and I always pretended, even with each other and no one else looking, that everything was fine.

But I miss *her*.

I miss moments like watching TV together while Dad was at meetings or on visits, the way she always had a little comment about Melinda Ford, or how she'd absently rub Ralph's stomach with her bare foot and he'd purr like crazy, so loud that she'd point the remote at him, pretending to turn him down. "Okay, Mister Cat. That's enough; you're embarrassing yourself."

I stand and say to Erin, "Be right back." She nods, focused on the news.

In the kitchen, the card for New Beginnings is tucked into the wall-mounted phone. She had to have gotten my message. New Beginnings isn't some giant place with hundreds of people. It's small and quiet and not chaotic, and every resident has a special cubby for messages and letters and boxes. So I know she got it.

While punching in the number, I have this image of her sitting on the edge of her dorm room bed, holding a piece of paper that says, "Call your daughter."

And then not doing it. Because . . .

I don't know why.

I hang up the phone on the first ring. Because what if I leave another message and she still doesn't call me?

"Hey, Sam," Erin calls, "your dad's on the news."

I can see the TV from the kitchen, but not very well. I get closer.

"It's from yesterday," Erin says, turning it up. "At the search. This was on last night, too. They're replaying a clip."

Melinda Ford stands in front of the media tent I saw yesterday, wearing different clothes, obviously, from what she had on in the live report she just did. She's asking my dad what parents should say to their children about Jody being gone.

"There are no magic words," Dad says, "but it's especially important in times like this to let your kids know that you love them, and that they're safe. I understand it's difficult. My own daughter, Sam, is friends with Jody, so we're very close to this situation."

At first I'm not sure I hear him right, but Melinda Ford repeats it, nodding her head, a concerned look on her face. "Your daughter is Jody's friend?"

"I'm not friends with Jody," I say to Erin.

I feel her eyes on me as Melinda keeps talking on the TV.

"And how is she coping with all of this?"

I watch, eager for the answer.

"She's out there searching right now, for one thing. Like all of us, she feels helpless." If Erin weren't hogging the remote, I'd turn Dad off.

"Pastor Charlie, what would you say to Jody right now if she could hear you?" Melinda holds the microphone to his mouth. Confident, he speaks right to the camera, his fingers interlaced in front of his chest. His sermon stance.

"Don't lose faith, Jody. We love you. God loves you. And love drives out fear, so don't be afraid."

My eyes burn. I grab the remote from Erin and change the channel, then throw it on the sofa and go to my room.

"Sam?" she calls after me.

I say it again, "I'm not friends with Jody." And close my door.

From the hall, she says, "You are. I mean, you kind of are."

How many times have I begged him not to use my name, my life, in public? I don't want to be a part of his act anymore. And love can't be the answer to everything. If it was, us loving Mom should have kept her from falling apart. Her loving us should have made her want to change.

I've paid enough attention to his sermons to know that what Dad said wasn't exactly right. *Perfect* love drives out fear, is what it says in the Bible. Perfect love. And who, my dad included, really knows anything about perfect love? Anyway, if God loves Jody so much, how could he let this — whatever it is — happen to her? And what else is he going to let happen to me?

"Sam?" Erin says again.

"Leave me alone," I say through the door.

After a minute, she says, "I know how you feel."

"I don't think so."

"My family has problems, too."

I could open the door and say, okay, what are your family's problems? And talk about it, and maybe she could help. But the only person I want to talk to right now is my mom.

"I'm going to lay down again," I say, resting my head on the door. "I'm just . . . really tired."

It's quiet on the other side and I think she's gone back to the living room, but then there's a soft, "Okay. Holler if you need anything." A moment later: "You could try writing a letter. To your mom.

Not one that you would send but one to have for yourself, you know? The stuff you can't say."

I run my fingers along the bevel of my door, picking up dust as I go. Finally, I hear Erin walk away, saying, "Come on, kitty," to Ralph, and making kissing noises at him.

Turning up the floor fan, I sit at my desk with a piece of binder paper and a pen in front of me. I stay exactly that way for about an hour, then go to bed.

Day 5

Wednesday

The national news has picked up Jody's story. I sit on the sofa eating cereal, watching pictures of Pineview and interviews with and about people I know. All this in the same hour that they talk about movie stars and the President. There's a shot of Main Street, deserted, with wavy lines of heat coming up from the pavement. Even though I was just there two days ago, it looks as foreign to me as if I were watching pictures of a town in Russia.

Suddenly everyone in the country is an expert on Jody. A guy with slick hair and a tweed blazer, from a university back east, is saying that Jody probably ran away, that there's probably an older boyfriend from another town, probably someone she met online.

"This is why we don't have Internet at home," my dad says from behind me. I twitch, startled, my spoon rattling against my bowl.

"Jeez, Dad. Don't sneak up on me like that." I haven't seen him since he left for the Shaws' house yesterday, without saying goodbye. Or saying hello again when he got home, apparently. So either it was really late or I slept like a rock.

"Sorry." He comes around and sits next to me. "You look a lot better. Erin says you had a good talk last night."

I look at him. Why is my life up for discussion between him and Erin? And I wouldn't say we had a "good talk." She talked and I had a good listen. I set my cereal bowl down on the carpet and Ralph comes over to lap up the milk I've left behind.

"Jody doesn't have an older boyfriend," I say. "Or any boyfriend. There's no way." If the "expert" could have seen Jody working on the glitter Jonahs, he'd know this.

"Maybe not. But —"

"Shh." I turn up the TV with the remote. Brandy Wilcox, a soap star who grew up here, Pineview's only claim to fame — until now, I guess — is on the screen. She's putting up $75,000 for anyone who has information leading to Jody's safe return.

"Oh, she called the Shaws last night," Dad says when the story is over. "So did Jody's father's old college roommate. He works for a regional FBI office and is on his way here to help."

"That's good, right?"

"It definitely doesn't hurt. Listen, Sammy." He hesitates. That moment of hesitation and the way he says my name means this won't be good.

I watch Ralph hunched over my bowl, his gray fur coming up in unruly tufts around his shoulders.

"With everything that's going on," Dad continues, "I don't like leaving you alone so much. It looks like I'm basically becoming the Shaws' official spokesperson. There are so many media requests and intrusions on their privacy, you wouldn't believe. They don't want to pay some stranger to handle this stuff, and they shouldn't have to when they've got their church family. And until they catch this guy . . ."

"You're sending me away?"

"No, not *away*, away. Honestly, Sam, I want to. But we can't afford a ticket to Grandma's, and she can't afford a ticket here. And you know the Hathaways love you."

I look at him. "You're making me live with Vanessa?"

He laughs. "You say that like I'm sending you to Siberia. It's not even two miles away, and she's your best friend."

"Did you check with Mom?"

"Check with her?" he asks, puzzled.

"Check with her." I get up and take the bowl away from Ralph. He isn't quite done, and races after me into the kitchen. "Discuss," I say over my shoulder. "Like, call her and say, 'I'm thinking about having Sam live with Vanessa until this is over and what do you think about that?'"

"I don't think we should bother her."

"How do you know? Have you even talked to her in the last week?"

I run the water, hard, to rinse my bowl, drowning out his silence. When I turn around, he's coming in with his coffee cup. "I didn't feel like it was a decision I needed help with. They've got cable, air-conditioning, home-cooked meals, they love you, you love them . . ."

But it's not home.

That's what Mom would have said to him, what she would have known about me and where I need to be right now. Sober, tipsy, drunk, whatever, she's the one who's been here, and she's the one who really knows me.

I fold my arms. "Why did you say on the news me and Jody are friends?"

"What?"

"Don't talk about me on TV, okay?"

"All right," he says slowly, but I can see he doesn't get why.

I start to notice how clean the kitchen is. All the surfaces have been straightened up and wiped shiny. Mom's notes and papers and mail are gone. I look in the trash and see them underneath a wet pile of coffee grounds. It must have been Erin who threw them away, since I've already told Dad not to.

The sight of random slips of paper with Mom's handwriting on them, in the trash, water-stained and covered in coffee grounds, leaves yet another part of me crushed.

I reconsider Vanessa's. Home doesn't feel like home anyway, so why not leave.

"What about Ralph?" I ask. "While I'm at Vanessa's."

"I'll feed him."

"You'll forget."

"I promise I won't." He turns his hands palms-up, helpless. "I just don't know what else to do right now."

I pick up Ralph and scratch behind his ears. "Don't make me go today." I want to at least get started on my backyard project. I want time to think. Maybe try calling Mom again. "I'll go tomorrow."

"Sam . . ."

"Please?"

He nods, and glances at the clock on the coffeemaker. "I've got to go over to the office for a few hours, then to the Shaws'. Okay?"

"Go. I'll be fine here."

I walk toward Main, my flip-flops slapping against the hot side-walk. The streets are empty, just like the picture on the news this morning. It's not like Pineview is usually crawling with children or anything, but today they're noticeably absent. There are things out here, though, that weren't here before: blue ribbons. Tied onto trees, and fence posts, and mailboxes. Symbols that we're waiting for Jody to come home.

I pass a house with a few old ladies sitting on the porch, drinking iced tea and playing cards. One of them calls me over. It's Ida Larson, from church.

I cross the brown lawn and climb the porch steps.

"Does your father know you're out wandering the streets?" Ida ruffles the hem of her blue print dress, fanning the air up her legs.

"I'm just going to the hardware store."

Ida and one of her card-mates exchange a glance. "Cal Stewart," she says. "New in town. Bought the store from the Penfolds three years ago."

Three years' residency is "new in town" here, especially to people like Ida. She's suspicious of everyone and always calls our house if her Sunday offering check isn't deposited by Tuesday morning. "I don't want my signature out there floating around where gosh-knows-who-all can see it, forge it, and take me for every penny."

"How's your mother, sweetie?" Ida asks now.

"Fine."

While Ida watches me, the rest of them look at their cards. "You just tell her that the Lord doesn't give a person more than he knows they can bear."

Ida Larson knows? Then everyone must know.

"Yes, ma'am."

My cell phone, in my shorts pocket, rings. I pull it out. "It's my dad," I tell the ladies, and they all smile and nod, like of course it would be my dad because that's how in touch we are with each other and isn't it great how Pastor Charlie is young and modern? "Have a nice day."

I go down the steps, and hit the button on my phone that will send my dad to voice mail, then slide it open as I walk away, pretending to talk. Even though he didn't explicitly say I couldn't go anywhere, I pretty much implied that I'd be locked up safe at home. Not answering his call saves me a lie.

Two blocks later I'm standing in front of the hardware store, watching Cal crouch in the window arranging a display of fans and garden hoses and potting soil.

I let my hand rest on the door for a second, staring at the flyer of Jody taped to the glass. It's the same picture they put on the TV this morning and now the whole country has seen her smiling face, full of braces.

When I go in, the strand of bells Cal has hanging on the handle jingles. His voice comes from the window: "Be right with you."

There's an end display of citronella candles and yellow jacket traps. I straighten them and wish I had a dust cloth or something. The store is a little sad right now, neglected. One thing you could say about the old owners is that they kept it clean.

"Oh," Cal says when he comes out and sees me. "The resident xeriscaper."

He wears a store apron with his name embroidered on the pocket, his wire-rim glasses resting on the top of his head.

"Yeah, well." I pick up a tube of cream that claims to be both a sunblock and a mosquito repellent. "Does this stuff work?"

"I've never tried it, but I don't see why it wouldn't."

I put the tube back. "Um, you know that plastic sheeting I got on Saturday?"

"Yes?" He's half-looking at a clipboard.

"I'm not sure exactly what I'm supposed to do with it."

"Cover up the lawn or weeds or whatever plants you want to kill." He looks up and smiles briefly. "Not much to it."

"How long does it take?"

"Depends. On the weather, on the types of plants. I'm sure you can find information online."

Online. Of course. Everything is online, only I'm not allowed online, but I'm too embarrassed to tell him that. "Thanks."

"No problem."

He wanders off with his clipboard. Still trying to work out a plan for the yard, I look at the rack of seed packets. The pictures of the flowers on the packets make it look so easy: dig hole, insert seed, water, and voilà — beautiful, colorful flowers.

Two summers ago there was a heat wave almost like the one we're having now, but my mom and dad planted our garden anyway, putting in the butterfly bushes and hollyhocks together. Dad laid the flagstone path. They bought yard furniture. It wasn't like last summer, when the good days were few and far between. This was a months-long stretch of togetherness. They'd let me stay up late into the night so I could sit with them out there, watching the stars. My mom seemed so happy. Open. Even the way she wore her hair back then told you something, always off her face so you could see her eyes smiling out at you.

I wish I understood what happened between then and now. I wish there was a way to put your finger on the map of life and trace backwards, to figure out exactly when things had changed so much: when we started getting the dregs of Dad, if that was before or after the drinking getting bad. If one caused the other, or if it was true what they say about it not being anyone's fault but instead genetics, or fate, or whatever you want to call it. My great-grandpa was an alcoholic, and sometimes my grandma in Michigan doesn't know how to stop once she starts. Still, it doesn't explain how one summer there were real smiles and yard projects and watching the stars together, and then what seemed like minutes later the yard and everything else were a total mess.

"Wildflowers do pretty well in the heat," Cal says from behind the register. "The ones on the rack should be right for this region."

"Oh," I say, turning, "I didn't bring money. I'm just kind of . . . looking."

He opens the register. "I'm sure I can advance you a couple of dollars. Just have your folks take care of it next time they're in."

There's only one folk right now, I want to say, and he's trying to get me out of the way so he can focus on the truly important stuff. Like Jody and her family. "Are you sure?" I ask.

He nods. "Pick one and take it, it's fine." I take a packet of seeds for flowers that look small and undemanding, and bring it to the register so that he can make up an IOU.

"Thanks." I turn toward the door to leave.

When I'm almost there, he calls after me. "Be careful out there."

"I will."

And I leave the store, the bells jingling behind me.

Back at home, I lie on my parents' bed, under the ceiling fan. I roll to my mom's side, smelling her pillow, but whatever trace of her there'd been is aired out and washed out. I stare at my cell phone for a long time, the New Beginnings card next to me on the blanket. Maybe there's a good reason she can't call me, like she's in group meetings and counseling and whatever else they make you do in rehab.

Even if there is a good reason, and honestly I can't think of one, it still hurts.

I had all these big plans for the yard today but now that I'm home I can't get myself up and doing anything. Gravity is powerful. It's still before noon, and I already slept like twelve hours last night, but my eyes want to close and I let them.

Pretty soon, I'm asleep.

I dream of Jody. She's in a hole in the ground, looking up. All I can see is her dirty, looking-up face, and there's no one around but me. No context, no sense of if I'm in Pineview or in a forest or a desert. Just me, Jody, and the hole. I lower a ladder. But instead of Jody climbing up, I climb down. We're both in the hole, staring at each other. She looks older than her picture on the flyer; her braces are off. She holds out her hand. I grab it. And then I wake up.

In the yard, I struggle with the black plastic sheeting, which I probably shouldn't be doing since it's early afternoon, the hottest part of the day. My cell phone rings. It's Erin.

"Ah-ha," she says when I answer. "Your dad suspected you might answer if it was me and not him."

I move into a shady spot, kicking the pile of sheeting into a manageable lump. "You're with my dad?"

"I'm at the office. Just taking care of some youth group business. Speaking of which, we're getting together tonight at Vanessa's to bake brownies and take them over to Nick's. It's the best we could think of right now."

It's easy to see how this will go: Dad takes me to youth group, and since it's at Vanessa's he'll say why don't I just pack a bag to stay over, thereby denying me the one more night at home he promised me this morning. Which somehow feels important.

"I'm still not feeling super great," I say. "I should probably stay home."

"It will not be strenuous, I promise. And you'll be well fortified because I'm going to cook you guys dinner."

"You're cooking dinner for the whole youth group?"

"No no, just for you and your dad . . . Here, I'm going to put you on speaker."

"Hey, Sammy." My dad sounds upbeat, energetic, and not mad that I didn't answer his call earlier. "How's your day?"

"Fine." I sit on one of the dirty plastic patio chairs, trying to think of what I can tell him I've been doing all day since I probably shouldn't mention going out, assuming Ida Larson hasn't already called him to squeal. "I'm just —"

But he cuts me off. "Here's the plan: I'm leaving the office now to check in with the Shaws. Then I'll come home, and Erin is going to bring us dinner at six, and afterward you guys will go do brownies at Vanessa's."

"And she'll bring me home?"

"Sure," Erin says.

Church people only bring meals to other church people when something is wrong. When people are "going through a hard time," as Erin always puts it whenever us youth group kids do meals for people. Casseroles when Heidi Capp's dad had cancer. Soup after the Fletchers had triplets. Brownies for Nick. And dinner for us — motherless and wifeless us.

"We don't need you to cook dinner," I say.

My dad laughs and says loudly, "Yes, we do! Pay no attention to the child!" They sound like they're having so much fun. I watch Ralph pounce on a butterfly.

"Dad, I can cook." Which I know is a direct contradiction to our conversation at the grocery store, but I can at least make some instant rice and open a can of fruit cocktail or something.

"I'm bringing food," Erin says. "Don't even worry about it."

"Can you take me off speaker? And let me talk to my dad?"

"Oh, okay."

He comes on the line. "Everything all right?"

"I don't know if I want to go to youth group tonight. I might be coming down with something." I move my flip-flopped toe over the plastic sheeting. Saying I'm sick could go either way in terms of trying to get him to change his mind about me moving to Vanessa's. He might just say it's better to be where Mrs. Hathaway can take care of me. Or he might decide to take care of me himself.

"Wait and see how you feel tonight. You'll probably want to go out after being cooped up all day."

I don't know how many different ways to say that I just want to be home.

"Sam?" he asks. "Still there?"

"Yeah. Okay." I slide the phone shut. Two black ants crawl across my toe and I let them, because right now I'm distracted with wondering if I should worry about my dad and Erin. I like her. Everybody does. Some of the youth group kids are really close to her, like she's a sister or an extra parent. If I could find the words to open up to anyone, I'd definitely consider her. But there's this one memory I can't get out of my head. Back in May, we had a mission trip–planning meeting thing at our house, a dinner. Mom was still able to pull herself together enough to pose as the perfect pastor's wife, cooking a bunch of Martha Stewart hot and cold appetizers and making punch. Everyone kept saying how good everything was, how great the house looked, how cute the little mice she made out of strawberry halves were, each tiny chocolate nose smelling its own miniature hunk of Swiss cheese.

What they didn't know was how I'd been helping for days, giving Mom pep talks every two hours, telling her it was going to be okay, everything looked great, no one was going to look behind the shower curtain and see the little bit of grime that might be in the corner of the tub and if they did they wouldn't judge her for it.

"You'd be surprised, Sam," she said, scrubbing out the inside of the microwave. "Some day, you'll know how it feels. There's a lot of pressure on a woman. Like you have to be camera-ready at all times. It hangs over you constantly, like homework you can't ever get an A on."

The people at the dinner also didn't know that she had her personal supply of punch under the sink, spiked with gin. I went in and out of the kitchen all night, making sure she was okay, making sure people had everything they needed, and one time I walked into the living room with a tray of mini quiches. Erin — who sat on the floor near my dad — was looking up at him, laughing, her eyes dazzling and alive, while he stared down at her, the biggest smile on his face. Everyone was laughing, not just them. You could tell that someone had just said something funny. Still, the look between them, something about it stopped me. It was the way I wished my mom and dad looked at each other. Everything else in the room disappeared as I watched them, until Daniel saw me standing there and said "Mini quiche!" and broke the spell.

And I don't think anything is going on. I'm sure it's not. If my mom doesn't think my dad is the kind of man who would cheat, why should I. But I will be paying attention.

Dad is barely home for twenty minutes when the doorbell rings a little before six. He shouts at me to answer the door — he's just getting out of the shower.

Erin looks excited to see me, even though she was just here yesterday. "Let me put this down, then I'm giving you a hug." She walks past me, smelling citrusy and dressed like she's stepped out of an outdoor supply catalog: cargo skort, athletic sandals, microfiber T-shirt, ponytail, and no makeup. That's her look, like she's ready to hit the climbing wall at a second's notice.

I follow her to the kitchen. "What did you make?"

"Patience, patience." She drops her keys on the counter, and sets down a foil-covered bowl and a grocery bag. "Hugs first. You look a billion times better than you did yesterday."

I let her give me her solid, full-bodied hug but now I'm on watch, and can't quite show much enthusiasm in return, especially as

I'm imagining her giving that same hug to my dad. Our church is touchy-feely, and my dad is among the most-hugged of the congregation.

"Homemade potato salad," she says, "cold grilled chicken, and fresh green beans. Sound good?"

"Fantastic," Dad says, and we both turn to see him there in the kitchen with us. His hair is damp, and he's wearing the brown polo shirt my mom says brings out the blue in his eyes.

I study Erin's face. Her cheeks could be going pink from whatever feeling there could be between her and my dad, or it could just be that her skin is reacting to the lack of cool air in our house.

"Yeah, looks good," I say, to remind them both that I'm there, too. I lift the foil off the bowl and pick up a chunk of potato salad with my fingers. It's better than any potato salad my mom ever made, with bits of bacon and a sweet, mustardy dressing.

Dad gets down plates from the cupboard.

Erin opens the plastic container full of chicken. The smell of lemon and garlic wafts out, bringing Ralph in from wherever he's been lounging. Erin watches my dad put out three plates and says, "Oh, just two."

"You're not staying?" Dad asks. Disappointment is all over his face.

"I already ate. I need to run and get the brownie stuff. You guys eat."

"Are you sure?" Dad holds the extra plate. "I thought . . ."

"I'll be back in about half an hour to get you, okay, Sam?"

"Okay." I've decided I do want to go, if only so that I can do something for Nick, even indirectly.

"Erin, really, there's plenty," Dad says.

"Dad, she said *no*." It comes out harsh, more than I meant. I open the drawer to get forks and knives, and feel them both looking at me. Ralph looks, too, his ears going flat. "I mean, she has to get the brownie stuff."

"So, yeah." Erin waves her hand dismissively, then draws it through her hair. "I want you guys to have leftovers." She whisks her keys off the counter. "See you in a bit."

After the door closes, Dad quietly feeds Ralph and puts glasses on the table, and we sit down. I scoop a heap of potato salad onto my plate, saw off a third of a chicken breast, and take about six green beans. His cell rings. And of course he answers it.

"Hey. Yes. Uh-huh." He listens for awhile, moving potato salad around with his fork. "I think we can get it together by Friday. And if . . . mm-hmm. Exactly."

The food is really good, and I'm starving, but I make myself leave some behind as if I don't like it, imagining Mom watching and worrying that I like Erin's cooking more than hers.

When Dad gets off the phone, I ask, "When are we going to visit Mom?" We haven't been since the day we all went together to drop her off, and got the tour and a stack of pamphlets they print up for family and friends. Those are still sitting around here somewhere.

"That's kind of up to her," he says, like this is no big deal. "The counselor there said that sometimes people choose not to have contact with their loved ones until they've really settled in."

"It's been three weeks. Of a four-week program."

He sets his fork down. "I know. We can't make her."

"Have you even asked?"

"I've been a little busy, sweetheart."

I want to say: I *know*, but it's Mom. She's your *wife*. You've got time to sit around the church office joking with Erin.

But how can I complain? Jody's parents don't even know if their daughter is alive. At least we know where Mom is. I get up for water. When I press my glass against the ice maker in the fridge door, a grinding sound comes from inside the freezer, followed by a loud clunk, before the whole thing kind of shudders and goes dead. Half a cube of ice drops into my glass. I stare at it, feeling the tears building.

Why does everything have to be broken right now? I think of Job, in the Old Testament, who lost everything. He didn't just lose everything, God *took* everything away from him — his wife, his kids, everything he owned. Despite it all, Job kept on believing that God knew what he was doing. Well I don't. I hit the fridge door with my open hand, hard, and it's all I can do not to smash my glass onto the floor.

"Sam, easy," Dad says.

I turn around. I want him to give me answers, but I can't even ask the questions. And he just looks at me like I'm the one with issues.

What's the point of being a pastor if you can't tell when your own daughter needs help? I turn away and draw water from the tap, over my half-cube of ice, and take it to my room to change before Erin comes back.

She's mostly quiet on the ride over to Vanessa's. The dark clouds that have been clustering and dispersing for days have finally stuck around, sending a half-hearted drizzle onto the windshield. Erin rolls down her window; the car fills with the scent of wet asphalt. I consider mentioning how Job-esque my life feels right now, but the response seems obvious: at least I'm better off than the Shaws.

"I love that smell," she says, dangling her arm out, opening and closing her left hand as if she could somehow grab hold of the thick evening air. "It reminds me of being your age. School out, running around in the streets with my friends, standing outside the house where my crush lived hoping he'd look out his window at exactly the right moment."

It's not hard to picture Erin as a teenager. She's only twenty-six now, and seems to remember what fifteen felt like, which is why she's good at what she does. And she is. It's easy to see why my dad likes being around her. Classy and elegant are words to describe my mom, and she's beautiful, but also she's anxious. A little high-strung. Erin is the opposite. Maybe when my mom was twenty-six, she was more like Erin, too. I wonder what my mom was like at fifteen. Like me, maybe, quiet, not sure where I belonged. I'd like to be like my mom when I'm older, with a little bit of a personality like Erin's mixed in.

In a flash, the drizzle turns into sheets of rain that hit the roof of the car with a sound like machine-gun fire. "Holy downpour, Batman," Erin says, frantically rolling up her window. "Sam, I know you don't really want to come do this tonight, but just remember these are your friends."

"Sort of," I say, as the car glides to a stop in front of Vanessa's house.

Erin makes a sound that's half laugh, half disbelief. "Why would you say that?"

She's observed us closely enough. She has to know that when they get together at non-church-sanctioned events — driving up to one of the alpine lakes in the summer to lay around and drink beer, or in winter meeting up at someone's house to watch horror movies or listen to music — they don't invite me. Even Daniel and Vanessa sometimes go to those parties and don't tell me. They're just "busy" and then I'll catch them talking about it and changing the subject when I appear. She has to realize that I'll never totally be one of them.

Anyway, I don't want to get them in trouble by telling all this to Erin. It will only confirm their idea of me as naive and goody-goody, or worse, a mole. So I say, "I just mean I'm shy."

"Well, we can work on that." She opens her door. "Come on."

I can see into Vanessa's living room as we walk across the brush in front of her house, crickets hopping away from our feet. Her house has an open floor plan, like ours. At least half the youth group has already congregated. Paul and Daniel and Allie are huddled with Kaleb Franklin around Kacey's iPod, Vanessa's mom passing through the kitchen with a pitcher of iced tea or punch or something, Daisy trying to show everyone her hedgehog chew toy.

"Ready?" Erin asks as we stand on the porch.

I nod, and we go in. The last time the youth group got together on a non-Sunday was before most of them went on the mission trip. Nick had been there, I remember, playing Guitar Hero with Daniel. For some reason that memory makes me so sad, like it's just another thing that will never happen again, because how can you sit around playing video games, that carefree, once you know how life really is?

Vanessa immediately runs over to give me a hug and grabs my arm, pulling me into the thick of things. Daisy tries to stand and put her front legs on my shoulders.

"Daisy, down," Mrs. Hathaway says, dragging Daisy by the collar. "I'm going to put her downstairs. You kids let me know if you need anything."

"We missed you in Meh-hee-co," Paul says, putting his skinny arm around my shoulder. Vanessa claims Paul has a crush on me, which only makes me want to avoid him because I don't know what to say to someone who has a crush on me. Like it isn't hard enough for me to relax and talk to boys, other than Daniel.

I let Paul side-hug me, anyway, and then Kacey comes over and hugs me, too. "Glad you're okay," she says. For someone who only comes to church because her parents make her, she seems pretty happy to be here, tonight.

"Thanks."

Erin holds up her grocery bags and says, "We should get started." She organizes us into brownie-making teams, and we get to work. They all have stories about the mission trip, shared experiences, inside jokes. Eventually, conversation tapers off while we concentrate on tasks. Until Allie, cracking eggs into a mixing bowl, says, "Are we *all* going to take these over to Nick? Tonight?"

Kacey grimaces. "It might be kinda overwhelming if we all just showed up on his porch, like, hi, hope you don't mind ten people dropping by with no warning or anything during this tragic time."

"We could call," Vanessa says. "It doesn't have to be with no warning."

Daniel, who's just put a handful of chocolate chips in his mouth, says, "Plus, we'll have brownies. Who doesn't want people showing up with homemade brownies?"

Everyone kind of laughs, but Paul says, "I may be crazy but I don't think brownies are going to cut it as a substitute for Jody."

We all stop what we're doing, Jody's name hanging in the hot air of the crowded kitchen. I glance at Daniel, who looks stricken. "Dude, that's not what I meant. At all."

"Okay," Erin says. "Let's think it through while the brownies cook."

Daniel leaves the kitchen, shaking his head. I set down the pan I've just coated with cooking spray and follow him through the dining room and down the hall. Without turning around, he says, "I hope you're not going to follow me all the way into the bathroom. 'Cause that'd be weird."

"Don't pay attention to Paul," I say to Daniel's back. "No one thinks that's what you meant."

He turns around, eyes red and watery, a smear of chocolate on his T-shirt, which is stretched tight across his stomach. "It was stupid of me to stay that. I was trying to be funny. It's a reflex. God, I'd be the worst pastor in the history of the world."

"No. Don't say that."

He wipes his hand over one eye, and leans against the wall in the hallway. "I don't know if you know, but Erin told us about your mom. I mean, I knew something was up. But she told us officially. I thought you'd want to know."

I blink. "When?" I shouldn't be surprised. It's never really been a secret. We just don't talk about it. Those aren't the same things. Every day I'm realizing a little bit more that I could have been talking to my friends about it all along.

"She sent out an e-mail last night. Seriously, Sam, when is your dad going to let you have e-mail? You miss a lot."

"What did it say?"

"Um, not to talk about it unless you brought it up. That it was a hard time for you. Pray for you. All the usual stuff."

I nod.

"So . . . do you want to? Bring it up?"

I try to smile. "You already did."

"Oh, yeah. Clever how I did that, huh?"

"Very. That skill will come in handy in your future career."

My little joke doesn't succeed in making him forget what we're talking about. "So you *don't* want to bring it up," he says.

I shake my head no. "Anyway, it doesn't matter right now. We need to focus on Jody."

"I can't even think about Jody. When I got home after the search on Monday I ate like a whole chicken and a bag of chips just to give me something to do other than think about Jody. If I don't keep making jokes I'm seriously going to start crying and never stop and that's not cool for me. She's just this sweet, goofy kid, like . . ." He puts his hand over his eyes. "Oh, man. Please, say something to keep me from breaking down. Or go get me a pound of chocolate chips. Punch me in the head. Kick me in the crotch. Anything, because I don't want to feel this."

There's got to be something I could say to him that would matter in this moment, but my brain has seized up. Because he's right. It's too much.

"Like, the brownies," he continues, uncovering his eyes. "What are we supposed to say to Nick? I don't even want to go over there. I can't look at him. Oh, crap . . ." He clutches his stomach. "Unless you want to be struck down by the toxic cloud of my puke, you should go away now." He runs into the bathroom and slams the door. I walk back down the hall, running my fingers along the textured wallpaper until I can see the kitchen, where everyone is quiet. Waiting, I guess, for me and Daniel to come back.

Erin catches my eye. "Is he okay?"

I shrug. I mean, obviously, no, none of us are okay.

"I should have kept my mouth shut," Paul says.

"I'm sure he'll let you off the hook," Erin replies. Then she turns to me. "Sam, they voted that you and I take the brownies to Nick."

Allie makes a bunch of noise with the mixing bowls. She's had a thing for Nick all year, but it's hard to believe anyone would see this as an opportunity for flirting.

"Why me?" I ask.

"You're least likely to say something lame and embarrassing," Kaleb says. They know I'm probably least likely to say *anything*. "We figure some of your dad must have rubbed off, somehow."

Well, it hasn't, is what I want to say. Daniel comes back in, looking pale and clammy. "Hey, man," he says to Paul. "Sorry for being an ass. Um, a jerk."

Erin checks her watch. "We've got eight minutes until the brownies are done. It wouldn't be the worst idea in the world for us to pray."

Each slat of the picket fence in front of the Shaw house has a blue ribbon tied around it. Stuffed animals and flowers and handwritten signs and cards completely cover the front porch. I bend down to pick up a teddy bear that's fallen off the pile and onto its side.

Erin exhales loudly. "Every time I come to this house, it hits me all over again. When you're standing right here you can't pretend it didn't happen."

I reposition the teddy bear, thinking about what to say to Nick, and what expression I should have on my face. Is it wrong to smile? I tighten my ponytail and take the brownie platter from Erin so that I have something to do with my hands. She rings the bell. Maybe we won't even see Nick. Maybe it will be one of Jody's parents I have to look in the eye, and that would be even worse.

But the man who answers the door is a stranger, to me at least, an older man leaning on a cane. "Oh, hello again," he says to Erin.

"Brownie delivery," she says. I hold up the plate. "From the youth group. They all wanted to send their love to Nick. Is he home?"

He opens the door wider.

"Come on in."

"This is Pastor Charlie's daughter, Sam," Erin says. I half-smile.

"Nice to meet you, Sam, I'm Ron. Jody's grandpa."

"Hi." I hadn't thought about grandparents. And there are probably cousins and aunts and uncles, too, a whole devastated family.

"We don't want to bother you," Erin says. "But we could visit a little if he's up to it."

"I'm sure Nick would be glad to see you." We follow him in and he turns and speaks low. "We'll just keep our voices down. Trish and Al are sleeping. First time in a couple of days. They kind of hit the wall this afternoon after you and Charlie left and are finally getting some rest."

"We can just leave these if that's better," Erin whispers, glancing up the stairs.

He waves his cane. "No, no. Nicky is up. The distraction will be good for him. Be right back." He goes up the stairs slowly, gripping the wooden railing.

I set the brownie platter on the coffee table; Erin sits on the sofa. The Shaws' house is older than ours, more interesting and kind of Victorian, with a high-ceilinged formal parlor where we are now. Pictures of Jody and Nick and their parents and other relatives line the piano and mantel. Some of the pictures have been featured on the news — I recognize one of Jody on a beach somewhere, smiling into the camera, showing off a sand dollar. I touch the frame.

"I love that picture," Erin says.

It's a good picture. But all I can think is how every day the girl in that picture becomes less real. The more she's on TV and on flyers and represented by blue ribbons, the more the real Jody — the one in choir, the one who lives . . . or lived . . . in this house — disappears. How long before the real person is permanently changed into a memory?

"Hey."

I turn to see Nick coming down the stairs, a small white dog trailing behind him. Erin stands to give Nick a hug, up on her toes since he's about a foot taller than her. When he lets go of her, he looks at me. "Hi, Sam."

He needs a haircut and probably about twenty hours of sleep, but other than that he seems like himself, barefoot and dressed in cargo shorts and a Lakers T-shirt. "Hi," I reply, bypassing the moment when we would have hugged by pointing to the brownies. "The youth group just made these."

"Thanks." He picks one up.

"Let me go grab some napkins," Erin says, and heads off toward what I guess is the kitchen.

"You want to sit down?" Nick asks me, indicating an armchair near the piano.

I sit, and the little dog comes over to sniff my legs. I reach to pet it. "Probably smells my cat. What's his name?"

"Her. Noodle." Hearing her name, Noodle goes over to Nick, who's still standing there with his brownie. "She's been looking for Jody. I think that's actually one of the hardest things for my mom . . . seeing Noodle running around the house, all frantic, smelling Jody everywhere."

He crouches and scratches Noodle's head, then looks at me with a kind of startled expression, like he's just noticed who I am, that I'm here. "Thanks for coming. It's been awhile, huh?"

I could point out that we only just saw each other on Sunday, but since then time has stretched and bent in strange ways so I know what he means. "I was going to come over with my dad a couple times, but . . ." I'm unsure how to finish that sentence. But I was too chicken? Too selfish?

Erin comes back in with some paper towels and two glasses of milk. "I took the liberty," she says, handing us each a glass. I sip from mine, watching Nick finally take a bite of his brownie, then another, then finishing it off with a third and gulping down most of his milk before wiping his mouth with a paper towel.

Realizing we're staring, he says, "Really good," and picks up another one.

I glance at Erin, thinking we should leave or be saying something meaningful, or do something other than watch Nick eat. The youth group was wrong, obviously, about my dad rubbing off on me.

Nick saves us by picking up the plate of brownies and holding it out to me. "Go ahead. I can't eat all these. I mean, I can, but I shouldn't. And we're not exactly having a food shortage here with people bringing stuff constantly." I take one.

Something about the way he offers the brownie reminds me of when he asked me to dance at that wedding, his natural niceness coming through in unexpected ways, even at a time like this.

I bite into the brownie. It's good, and still warm. I think hard about what I could say to Nick. *I'm sorry about Jody* feels empty and seems to go without saying. Erin starts talking to him, and I watch his face. What would I want someone to say to me if a person I loved disappeared, and I didn't know where she was?

A person I love did disappear.

But it's different. Every future I imagine has my mom in it. Whereas Nick has to imagine possible futures without Jody, without that person who looks like you, and knows what it's like to be in your family. Possible futures as an only child.

"So, you know," Erin says to Nick, "we're all here for you, whatever you need." Her cell phone rings; she picks it up from where it's sitting on the coffee table with her car keys, and makes an apologetic face. "I should get this."

I eat another bite of brownie. Take a sip of milk. Pet the dog. Continue to say nothing. The Youth have no idea how much they should regret sending me.

"Can't the twins take you?" Erin is saying. "Well, did you ask? . . . Okay, give me a couple of minutes." She hangs up. "Allie needs a ride home. I can't let anyone walk or I'll be in deep doo-

doo." Looking at me, she says, "I don't want to rush you out, Sam. Why don't I go get Allie, run her home, and then come back for you?"

"Oh." I start to get up. "I can just go now." It's painful enough with Erin here, who at least is a kind of buffer.

"No," Nick says quickly, almost desperate. "Stay. I mean, you just got here."

I glance at Erin. *Please say you have to get me home.*

"Yeah, Sam, stay." She picks up her keys.

"You don't mind coming back for me?"

"Don't be crazy." And she gives Nick another quick hug — it's so easy for her — and walks out. Nick takes a third brownie. I look around the room at all of the pictures and cards, just to have something to do with my eyes other than look at him.

Forced to deal with a mute, he says, "Your dad's been really great. I don't know what we'd do without him."

"Oh. Yeah. Good."

Sometimes, moments like this, I can see my dad a little bit through other people's eyes. Objectively I can say he's a good man who cares about people, a good pastor who cares about his church. And I wonder if I expect too much. If I picture it as a giant scale, with me and Mom on one side, and the whole congregation on the other, Mom and I are way up there, light as feathers, compared to the weight of the rest of everyone else who needs him.

Nick leans back on the sofa, groaning and patting his stomach. "One brownie over the line."

I smile a little and set down my milk. "Yeah." I'm sure this conversation will go down as one of the worst in the history of Nick's life.

"Look," he says, "I'm sorry. I know this is . . . I should have let you go with Erin."

Even he realizes this is a disaster and wants to get rid of me.

He sits forward. "I just wanted to feel normal for a minute. Spending twenty-four hours a day with my parents and grandparents is definitely not normal."

I want to feel normal, too. "When do you leave for State?"

"I'm supposed to be packing up my room and stuff for moving into the dorms, like, right now. I can't do that to my parents . . . pack up and leave in the middle of this. But in my head I am. Sorting out my junk. What I'll take, what I'll leave." He glances toward the staircase and lowers his voice. "I want to leave, though. That's horrible, right? To want to bail? To want to just get out of here and be somewhere else?"

And that second, everything changes. Nick doesn't think I'm a disastrous, boring mute. We really are having a conversation. I just haven't figured my part out yet. Now is my chance to finally say something. "I don't think it's horrible. I think . . . probably anyone would want to be anywhere else."

"Yeah." He nods, like he expected nothing less of me than to understand. "You're right. Speaking of getting out of here, I can take you home, you know."

"Oh, I think I should wait for Erin."

"Call her," he says, already standing to get his keys off the side table and feel for his wallet.

I stand, too, and straighten my shorts, tighten my ponytail. I pull my phone out of my pocket and pause. I don't want Erin to say no, to say she's already on her way. In about three minutes I've gone from desperately not wanting her to leave me here alone to desperately not wanting her to come back. So I text her instead of calling: *Nick's taking me home.*

On our way out, Nick slides his feet into the sandals by the door and says, "Let me just tell my grandpa I'm leaving so that no one worries."

He jogs up the stairs, and I step out into the night to wait. Though the sun is down, the day's heat lingers, pulsating from gravel and through the thin soles of my flip-flops. It feels more like a regular summer night, and less like the backward world we've been living in since Sunday. And even though so many things are going wrong right now, I want something in me to still be able to enjoy a night like this, to feel that it's good to be here, and alive.

"Okay," Nick says, closing the door behind him and pointing to the silver mini-truck in the driveway. "You're the first passenger in my new ride. I just got it Saturday. It's five years old, but my last one was thirteen so it feels brand new to me."

I walk around to the front of the truck as Nick turns on the headlights, illuminating my legs and swarms of gnats. When I climb in, his cell rings. He flips it open while simultaneously backing out of the drive. "Hey," he says. "Nothing." He holds the phone to his shoulder with his head and puts the truck in gear to start us moving forward. "I can't."

The trees and houses and fences flick by as we gain speed, blue ribbons everywhere.

"I know," Nick says into the phone. "I'm sorry."

I find the button to lower the passenger window. The breeze dries my damp neck.

"Not sure," Nick says. "Dorrie —" Then he holds the phone out for a second, looking at it in disbelief before turning it off and folding it shut. He tosses it into the cup holder and accelerates, up-shifting as we hit the straightaway on Main. "My old car couldn't do this. It was a four-cylinder automatic. That's not driving." He glances at me. "Do you have your license yet?"

"Next year. My dad's supposed to teach me to drive this summer." I'm wondering how Dorrie Clark could hang up on Nick, especially with everything that's going on.

"The clock is kind of running down on 'this summer.'" He accelerates again. "Here. In about five seconds I'm going to put the clutch in and you're gonna put it in fourth. See the little diagram here?" He taps the stick shift. "Just follow the map. Ready?"

"Really? What if I break it?"

"You won't. One, two, three . . . now."

I touch the shifter tentatively. Then Nick puts his hand over mine, firm. "Straight down. There you go." He lifts his hand, completely unaware that it's as close to holding hands as I've ever come. He eases his foot off the clutch and now we're flying, the speed of the truck cooling down the air that blows through the open windows. "I wish we could take it out onto the freeway," he says. "But I guess I should get you home."

No rush, I want to say. But at the corner of Sagebrush and Main I tell him, "You can turn here to get to my house."

He stops but doesn't signal, letting the truck rock back and forth while he keeps one foot on the gas and one on the clutch. "Let's at least drive it back up Main. You can try the other gears."

A bead of sweat trickles down the side of my face, the air still again. I can see the hardware store up ahead on the next block, the window display lit up but the shop lights out.

"Just ten more minutes," Nick says. He must take my silence for hesitation, which it isn't. It's just silence. "Five. I don't want to go home yet. I really, really just don't want to go home."

I turn and study his profile the way I figure every girl who's ever known Nick has studied him. His face has perfect symmetry. Each feature works with the others: eyes set at the right width and depth, leading to the nose that's exactly centered and straight, leading to a dip above his mouth that you want to put your finger on, tracing it down to his wide lips and strong jaw. He could probably be a model.

"What?" he asks, looking back at me and smiling a little.

"We can keep driving for a while," I say. "Five minutes."

"Okay. Cool." The whole time we've been idling here, there's been exactly one car coming from the other direction, and one car behind us, which simply went around without beeping or anything. "When I tell you," Nick says, "ease it from first to second." We're in motion again. "Go."

I move the gearshift down.

"Good. Third is trickier. Follow the map."

I look at the shifter and try to maneuver into third gear. The truck makes a sick grinding noise.

"Whoa, whoa, not yet," Nick says. I jerk my hand away, and he laughs. "Wait for me to say when."

"Sorry."

"It's okay." He accelerates and puts in the clutch. "Now."

He puts his hand over mine again and we move the truck into gear, and it's so gentle, his hand, like when he danced with me that one time, and I don't know what to think. Two hours ago I barely knew Nick and now he's not moving his hand off of mine and his long fingers are curled over my shorter ones. We're just driving, I think, trying to ignore my tingling fingertips.

A car shoots out in front of us from nowhere. Nick takes his hand off mine to honk the horn and swerve to avoid a collision. I put my hand in my lap. "I should get home," I say, lightheaded.

"Yeah," he says reluctantly, "okay."

He turns the truck around and heads back to my house, and I'm thinking that I should say something meaningful about what's going on, something not canned or slight or stupid. But Nick talks before I think of anything. "Your mom. She's in rehab?"

I lean my head out the window a little ways to let the air cool my face.

Nick says, "Sorry. If you don't want to talk about it, that's cool."

"No, I . . . I just keep forgetting that people know." That life is never really private, that it's something other people look at and wonder about and make their conclusions based on what really might just be the tip of the iceberg.

"So, what kind of rehab? I'm going to be a psych major. That's the plan anyway. Hence my nosiness."

"Oh." Maybe that's why Nick wants to spend time with me. To probe my psyche about living with an alcoholic. "I'm not sure. It all happened kind of fast . . . she wrecked her car and got cited for a DUI and they kind of 'strongly urged' her to do this program. I don't think she would have otherwise."

"Wow. Your mom is so . . ." Perfect? "I just never would have thought." He slows in front of our neighbor's house. "This it?"

"The next one."

I feel us both noticing the blue ribbon tied to the tree in our front yard. It wasn't there earlier — I don't know who put it up.

The other thing we both notice is the little car behind my dad's. "Isn't that Erin's car?" Nick asks.

"Yeah." I try to say it like it's completely expected and okay for the single-girl-youth-group-leader's car to be in our driveway while my handsome dad is home and my mom is not. "Thanks for the ride."

"Next time, I'll let you get behind the wheel."

"Okay," I say, sincerely doubting there will be a next time, but make no move to get out. The truck engine idles. "Yeah. I guess I'd better go." Finally, I lift the door handle, push the door open, and swing my legs out.

"Hey," Nick says, stopping me. "If you ever need anything, give me a call."

Like what? He's the one in the middle of a real crisis. I nod. "Sure."

"No, really, I mean, I'm just here for . . . as long as it takes. I'm not working or anything because I thought I'd be leaving for school in a week. And I'm used to doing all kinds of stuff for Jody. Giving her rides or whatever. And now —" For the first time tonight, he looks like he might cry. "Anyway, I've got all these big brother skills. That's all."

Then, without thinking, I blurt, "Maybe they'll find her."

A car drives by, sweeping its headlights over Nick's face. His gaze is far away, his curly hair sticking out over his ears. Then the cab of the truck goes dark again. "We'd need a miracle," he says. "A real one. Do you think those happen anymore?"

I want to reach across the truck cab and touch him, and tell him that is the exact same question I've been asking myself for a long time now and I'm glad I'm not the only one wondering. Before I can move, the driveway lights come on and flood the truck. Nick shields his eyes and laughs. "Dang. What does your dad think we're doing out here?"

I scoot out of the truck and close the door. "Thanks again," I say through the open window.

He lifts his hands off the wheel. "See you, Sam."

The front door opens the second I reach it. My dad is standing there, Erin behind him, looking like she thinks she belongs. "Finally," Dad says.

"What took you so long? You texted me almost half an hour ago, Sam." Erin is aggravated. "It's a five-minute drive."

"We were talking." I squeeze past them and into the hot living room, where there are mugs on the coffee table and a plate of brownie crumbs. Ralph rubs himself against my legs.

"That's fine," Dad says. "But you need to let me know where you are, especially now."

"And keep your phone on when you're out," Erin adds.

I pull my phone out of my pocket. The display is black. I turn around to face them. "The battery must have died. I didn't know." Then I think about what she just said and the way she said it. Like she's my mom.

"Nick's phone was off, your phone was off . . . anyway, you're okay, so, phew." She turns to my dad. "Remember what I said, Charlie, okay? See you tomorrow."

"Okay." He smiles and nods. I follow his eyes following Erin as she leaves, her calf muscles flexing and shiny hair swinging.

"What did she mean, remember what she said?" I ask as the door closes.

"Oh, she offered to bring dinner over again sometime."

"I can try to cook."

He laughs and walks past me to lock the door for the night, something we never used to do. "So, what did you and Nick talk about?"

"I don't know. Is there any food left?" I head for the kitchen.

"You don't know what you talked about?" he asks, following.

"Stuff." I open the fridge. Erin's potato salad is still there. I push it aside to get out the grape jelly, butter, and bread, and put a slice in the toaster.

"Ah. Stuff. Well, next time I'd prefer it if you called me for a ride, or Erin, or Vanessa's mom."

I stare at the toaster. "Why? Nick offered. He didn't have anything else to do. He was lonely."

"Because. I'd just prefer it."

The toast pops up. I spread on butter and a thick layer of jelly. "That's not a reason. You told me you wanted me to spend more time with youth group people."

"Nick is barely in youth group. He's older. He's in college."

"Not yet."

"Sammy," he says in his don't-wear-me-out voice. "Just say you'll do as I ask."

I wrap a napkin around my toast and go past him toward my room.

"Sam?" he calls after me. "Samara?"

"Good night, Dad," I say, and close the door.

Day Six

Thursday

I stand over the stove, poaching an egg in the little pan that has four neat poaching cups, the one Mom used for eggs Benedict. Also, there's a peeled and sliced banana on a plate, a glass of milk, and a glass of orange juice. I want to show my dad that I do listen to what he says, and I can take care of myself and he doesn't need to make me move to Vanessa's.

But when he comes into the kitchen, his first words to me are, "You've got your stuff together?"

He's purposeful as he heads to the coffee pot, eager to check this off his to-do list.

"Not yet."

"I need to be out of here in forty-five minutes. I'm sitting down with the Shaws to plan the prayer vigil for tomorrow night. The press wants to come, and it's sort of a logistical nightmare." He dumps a full coffee filter into the trash and whips open a kitchen drawer to get a new one.

"What about Mom?" I ask, poking at the egg in the poaching cup. It's still jiggly.

"What?"

Hello. My mother. Your wife? "We were going to talk about planning a visit?"

He scoops coffee out of the can he keeps in the fridge. The spoon scrapes the bottom with a metallic ring. "Yes, we were." He measures out water. Turns on the pot. Thinking what to say next. "And we will. Let me get this prayer service out of the way and we will."

There's always something in the way. If you ask him for things on a Wednesday or after, he says let me get Sunday out of the way. Then Sunday is out of the way and he says let me catch up and recover, so basically Tuesday is the only day of the week he's not in recovery or needing to get something out of the way. And this has nothing to do with Jody. It's always like this.

But now, I'm taking matters into my own hands. Seeing Erin's car in our driveway last night and imagining seeing it there again has made me determined to get Dad to see Mom. To look at her, and remember who is who. "We could go get her after church on Sunday and go to the Lodge."

He sniffs at a carton of half-and-half. "Oh. Let's see what else is going on — a lot can happen between now and Sunday."

"The Lodge is practically halfway to New Beginnings, and we go almost every Sunday anyway. Let's just call her right now."

I turn off the flame under my egg and reach for the phone. Dad looks at his watch, but I think he knows he's out of excuses. I punch in the number and go through the automated menu to talk to a person, a man. "Is Laura Taylor available?"

"You can leave a message and we'll make sure she gets it."

"This is her daughter. I left a message before."

"Yeah, I think I got that message off the system. I delivered it myself."

"Are you sure?" I feel Dad's eyes on me, but I keep mine on the stove.

"Do you want to leave another message?"

I just want to hear her voice.

"Yeah. Tell her I called and she should call me back. About brunch on Sunday." I give him my cell number and make him say it back, in case there's any chance my mom forgot it. When I hang up I go straight to my egg to put it on the plate, but the whites stick to the poaching cup and by the time I get it out the whole thing is a mess. My eyes fill with tears but I'm making myself not cry, not cry, as I sit to eat.

I wish that for once, my dad, who always has the right words for everyone else, would have a clue what to say to me.

He does try to talk to me on the ride to Vanessa's, but not about Mom. "We never finished our discussion last night," Dad says.

"There are a lot of discussions we never finish."

"About Nick, Sam." He's not playing around. "I need to have your word that you won't see him without my permission." Which is more explicitly anti-Nick than what he said last night about not taking rides in general.

I say okay, just to end this. And also because Dad didn't keep his word about calling Mom, or about talking about our plan, or about half a dozen other things I can think of off the top of my head, including how he was going to teach me to drive this summer. I'm figuring out, finally, that it's easier to do what he does: give your word and then make up an excuse later.

When we pull up to Vanessa's, I can see her waiting on her wide front porch, swinging in the hammock, one foot on the ground, pushing herself back and forth. Daisy is underneath, napping. I start to climb out of the car and my dad says, "Sam, this is just for a few days. A week, tops."

How do you know? I want to ask. I don't know if he's saying he's confident Jody will be found, or he's confident she won't and then we'll go back to normal, or he's confident Mom will actually want to come home after her time is up even though she won't even return a phone call. The way things have been going, I don't know how he can be so sure about anything.

All I can do is nod. He touches my hair. I look at him. Considering everything, he might actually be doing his best. I'm disappointed but also know that if I really thought about it, I could probably come up with at least as many times he's kept his word as times he hasn't. Most of all I want to believe — in him, in God, in our family — the way I used to. It used to be that there was always one of them I could count on. If Dad was lost in his work, Mom and I had each other, even if it wasn't perfect. If Mom was lost in her drinking, Dad would pull us together and get us back on track. And I was always sure God hovered around there among us, somehow.

Right now it's like we're three islands, and nothing but oceans between us.

Moving into another family's house, even temporarily, is just one more thing to separate us.

"Let me help you take your things in," he says.

"I got it."

I lean over and give him a kiss, collect my stuff from the back seat, and close the door.

He drives off before I'm even halfway up the walk.

I drop my duffel bag and pillow onto the porch before petting Daisy hello and wedging in next to Vanessa.

"Hey," she says, scooting over.

"Hi."

We sway back and forth for a little while, and even though I didn't want to come here, I'm starting to relax. "It's kind of nice out," I say.

"I know. For a change I'm not roasting like a Thanksgiving turkey out here."

There's a blue ribbon around the Hathaways' mailbox. When we're sitting out here two weeks from now, in a month, in a year, will the ribbons still be up? I wonder how you're supposed to know the exact moment when there's no more hope.

"How did it go at Nick's last night?" Vanessa asks.

"Okay. I mean, sad, but okay." I don't really want to share any of the personal stuff Nick and I talked about, or even that he gave me a ride.

"Did he seem . . . normal? Or, like, weird about Jody? Or anything?"

"He seemed sad, like I said."

She's quiet after that. Too quiet, for Vanessa.

I look at her. "What?"

She looks back, touches her neck. "I know you don't go on the Internet, but you'll probably hear about it anyway eventually."

"What?" I repeat.

"There's this whole big theory about Nick. Being . . . a suspect."

Without missing a beat, I say, "That's stupid." I can tell from her face and the tone of her voice that some part of her believes it could be true.

"I heard that the police confiscated his laptop," she says, as if that's evidence.

"They took *all* the computers in the house. I heard about it on the news, too. They just wanted to see if Jody had been talking to anyone online or whatever."

"Yeah, but . . ."

"Nick didn't do anything." I get up off the hammock, throwing Vanessa off balance so that she has to steady herself with her hands and move back to the center. Daisy gets up, too, and stands between us, tail wagging slowly. I pick up my duffel bag, ready to go inside.

"Well *I* don't think so, either," Vanessa says, "but they keep saying it's usually someone in the family and think how many times you've heard stuff like that on the news — how the person who does something horrible is the last you'd suspect."

"It wasn't Nick."

"Okay," Vanessa says guiltily. Then, with a burst of insistence, says, "But we don't really *know* him, do we? I was thinking about it and we see him at church on Sundays and sometimes at youth group stuff and around school but do we *know* him?"

"We've known him as long as we've known anybody. You might as well say it's Daniel, or my dad."

"That's not the same."

"It is, though. If you say it could be Nick, it could be anybody."

She stares up at me, eyes watery, and says, "That's what I mean, Sam. It could be anybody."

And I know what she means, what she's trying to get across. That a thing like this changes the way you think about everything and everyone, and you can never go back.

Mrs. Hathaway drives us to Daniel's in the afternoon to swim in his pool. Robby begs to go with us, but Mrs. Hathaway saves the day by offering to take him and any two friends he wants to the water park on Saturday instead.

We lay out in our suits, baking in the three thirty sun. Vanessa and I spent most of the day so far looking at all the Jody news on her dad's laptop, and now my head is cluttered with the rumors. And they aren't just about Nick. They're about Jody's dad, her uncle, her teachers, some random guy in Ohio. There are people all over the country who think they've seen her in their town. Someone in the boonies of Alaska says they saw her, and someone in Chicago says *they* saw her, on the same day. Already there are all these blogs and websites and message boards filled with theories and guesses and people just trying to figure this out. Finally I told Vanessa, "I don't want to look at this stuff anymore. It's crazy."

She closed the laptop and said, "I know. Every day I promise myself I'm not going to look, but then I do and I can't stop."

My dad not wanting me to be alone with Nick makes a little more sense, considering everything I saw online. Not that I think there's a remote chance it could be him, but I can see how easy it is to get paranoid.

Now Daniel and Vanessa are theorizing some more. "Maybe she did run away," he says. "Or maybe at first she was taken but now she has that thing. That syndrome."

"Stockholm," Vanessa says. "Stockholm syndrome."

"Yeah, that. And now she's like in a cult and we should leave her alone."

"I don't think you can get that so quick." Vanessa props herself up on her elbow. "And if she's in a cult, we should definitely not leave her alone. Cults are bad, remember? As a future pastor I'd think you'd know that."

He groans. "I wish I'd kept my fat mouth shut about the pastor thing."

I get up and slip into the pool, letting the water close over me. It's not as cool as I wish it were, but at least it's quiet, surrounding me with the white noise of the pool filter. I try to clear my head so it's as quiet as the pool, using an image of how I want our garden to look as a way to silence everything else. Then I hear a muffled splash and re-emerge. Daniel swims toward me, making a shark fin out of his hands, palms pressed together on the top of his submerged head. It's very sixth grade.

I paddle away from him for a few yards, then we both stop. He comes up out of the water, shaking his head, droplets of water staying on his pale skin — the skin of someone who spends more time with his computer than in the outdoors. "You okay?" he asks.

"No," I say, tiptoeing backward on the rough bottom of the pool, toward deeper water.

"Me, neither."

"Do you really wish you hadn't said anything about what happened to you in Mexico?" I tread water, letting the smooth, warm-ish waves of it churn over and around my arms.

"I don't know. I just know I want to do something . . . meaningful. I want to do what God wants me to do. And I thought it was that." He pulls a green pool noodle over and drapes his arms on it. "I didn't know there'd be all this extra stuff, whatever it is, when I tell people. They either look at me like I'm insane or start asking me deep theological questions about the meaning of life."

I wonder if that's how it feels to my dad, still. That everyone thinks he's crazy, or that he has all the answers. I just want him to have *some* of the answers. "Remember what my dad said. You could be God's Chosen Waiter."

"Yeah, well, your dad makes everything sound meaningful, and easy."

"It's an act." I dive under the water and come back up near the edge, intentionally splashing Vanessa. She squeals and sits up. "I think I'm starting to burn," I say. "Let's call your mom to pick us up."

KPXU
LIVE @ FIVE

The mood here in Pineview has turned somber as the fifth day of the search for Jody Shaw comes to a close. Several leads in the case have evaporated as quickly as they came and investigators are no closer to finding the thirteen-year-old, missing since Sunday. Police have said that no one, including family members, has been eliminated as a suspect but emphasize that the family has been cooperative. Regional FBI agents are working with local authorities; attempts to link Jody's case to those of two girls missing in southern Oregon have failed. Sympathy for the Shaw family was palpable at Library Square today as volunteers waited in line and local companies donated food and drinks to searchers. A tip line has been set up for those with any information about the case. The numbers are at the bottom of your screen.

Pineview Community Church will hold a prayer vigil tomorrow night at seven PM; people of all faiths are welcome.

This is Melinda Ford, reporting live from the KPXU studio.

"Mom," Vanessa says from her beanbag chair in front of the TV. "We have to go to that." She looks at me. "You want to, right?"

"Yeah," I say, even though really, I'm not sure.

"Of course," Mrs. Hathaway says. "We'll all go."

*   *   *

After dinner we sack out in a pile of pillows in the basement, eating ice cream while Robby plays video games. I've kept my cell phone close all day in case Mom calls. Or Dad. Or anyone. When we got back from Daniel's I called my own phone from the Hathaways', just to make sure it works. It does.

"This reminds me of the old days," Vanessa says.

"The 'old days,' like, last year?"

She looks at me. "No. I mean like the old days. Like when you used to be here every weekend. When your mom and dad would come for dinner, and you'd stay to sleep over, and we'd sit down here while they were up there."

And her dad would play his guitar, old songs from when they were all in high school, and they'd try to remember the words, and laugh so much.

"It wasn't *that* long ago," I say.

She puts her spoon down. "Yeah, Sam, it was. It was forever ago. And then you, like, disappeared. I mean, where did you go?"

I stare into my bowl, pushing the melting ice cream around. Vanessa is remembering our childhood, basically. And I understand why, I do. But like so many things, it's gone. "I don't know. Nowhere."

"You could have talked to me about your mom."

I glance at Robby, whose thumbs are working like mad on his game controller. "She didn't want people to know."

"It's not like I would have told anyone."

"I know." It's just hard, I want to say. The things that happen in your house, with your family, are personal. How do you talk about finding the spaghetti sauce lid in your dinner or the ice cube trays full of water in the towel closet? How do you talk about helping your mom put on her lipstick, so carefully, because her hands are shaking, so that it looks as perfect as she needs it to look before she can face the world?

All I can say to Vanessa is, "I'm sorry. Now you know. Now everyone knows."

She goes back to scraping her spoon in the bowl. "She'll come back and be a lot better. You'll have a fresh start."

I know the place is called New Beginnings, but I don't think it works quite like that. You can't just erase everything that came before.

Vanessa's mom calls down the stairs. "Robby, come on up and brush your teeth and get your pj's on."

He puts down the controller and switches off the game without protest. Such an easy kid. He gets to the bottom of the staircase before turning to me and saying, "Night, Sam. Your mom'll get better."

Of all the things people have said and not said to me over the last couple of days, this is the one that makes me want to cry. It's so unexpected, and Robby sounds so sure, the way only a seven-year-old can. I barely manage to get out a "Thanks, Robby," without my voice cracking.

Then, my cell rings; I lunge for it. I don't recognize the number, but I'm sure it's New Beginnings. "Hello?"

"Hey."

It's Nick.

"Oh," I say, surprised. "Hi."

Vanessa is watching me. "One sec," I say to Nick, then stand and tell Vanessa, "Be right back," before going upstairs and slipping into the guest bathroom at the end of the hall. "Hi."

"So, how are you?" Nick asks.

"Okay. How are you?"

"Um, you know. Bad." Then he kind of laughs, and it dawns on me that of course he'd know, too, all the stuff it says about him online. "Am I interrupting anything?"

"No. I'm just at Vanessa's."

"I can call you back later if you're busy."

I stare at myself in the bathroom mirror. There's a nice, soft light in here that makes my skin look good and my hair shiny. I wonder how Nick sees me. Just someone who can use his "big brother skills"? Or as a real friend?

"Actually," I say, watching the way my mouth looks when I talk. "I kind of moved in. Temporarily."

"Really? Why?"

"My dad thinks it's bad for me to be alone so much. And he's busy with . . . everything."

"Yeah. He's helping my parents a lot. Sorry."

"It's okay." I turn away from the mirror, still waiting for the reason he called.

"He and Erin just left here after working out stuff for the vigil thing," Nick says, "and I was just thinking about you. So I thought I'd call and say hi. How's your mom?"

"I don't know. I've left a couple of messages for her and she hasn't called me back." It's the first time I've said that out loud, and even though the truth of it feels bad, it's a relief to say.

"Oh. That's kinda . . . that sucks."

"She doesn't have to be there that much longer." Emphasis on the *have to*. She could stay longer, if she wants. "Maybe she's just trying to get through it."

"Maybe. But she should call you back. You're her daughter."

I gnaw on one of my knuckles. My stomach feels shaky. All I can say is, "Uh-huh." Because now my mind is stuck on what he said about how my dad and Erin just left his house, together. And I'm here. And our house is sitting there, empty.

"Sorry, you probably don't want to talk about it. I guess it's nice for me to talk about someone else's problems for a change but if you don't want to . . ."

After taking a deep breath, I say, "I guess I'll see you at the vigil?"

"Yeah. I'll be there. Come find me after, okay?"

"Okay."

When I hang up, all of Nick's words are running through my head. Until now, I've been convincing myself that Mom would have a good reason for not calling me, but there isn't one. There just isn't one. Like Nick said, I'm her daughter. And my dad is her husband. And he's with someone else right now. Maybe. Suddenly, I have to know for sure.

Panicked, I come out of the bathroom and run into Mr. Hathaway in the hall. "Um," I say, and he stops. "I'm really sorry but I left something at my house that I need."

"I can run you by in the morning to get anything you need," he says, smiling helpfully.

"I kind of need it tonight."

"Oh, well." He checks his watch. "You sure it's not something Vanessa or her mom can . . . supply you with for tonight? Did you check under the sink?" He thinks it's female products.

"It's not."

He feels bad for me for everything that's going on, I can tell, and doesn't press further. "Sure. Okay. Grab Vanessa and I'll take you."

In the Hathaways' minivan I try to stay calm and think about what I'll do if Erin's car is parked at our house. This was stupid. Because now if it's there, Vanessa and her dad will know, too. I think of what I could say. Like that they have a meeting about the prayer vigil or youth stuff. I'll pretend it's normal, I'll pretend not to notice it.

Before we left, Vanessa asked what we're getting. "Just something

I need," I told her. She looked at me funny but didn't ask for more. Now we're sitting in the back of the van and her dad has the AC up to the point I wish I had a sweater. It's not quite dark out yet, but getting there.

We turn the corner to my block. I crane my neck to see past Mr. Hathaway's head and get a glimpse of the house. There are no cars out front, not even my dad's, and I know there can't be any in the garage other than my mom's, which has been parked there since her accident and arrest. The driveway lights are on but otherwise the house looks empty. I blow breath out.

"You have your key?" Mr. Hathaway asks as he pulls into the drive.

"Yeah." I open the sliding door and climb out, then realize Mr. Hathaway and Vanessa are getting out, too. "Oh, I'll just be a second; you don't have to come in."

"No, no. Dad duty. I'm not sending you into a dark house alone."

"And I'm not sitting here by myself," Vanessa adds.

They follow me to the door. I hesitate, wondering where my dad is, anyway, if he's not here. Maybe they're at her house. Or maybe I'm just crazy for thinking anything could possibly be going on. Jody's family needs my dad right now, and they need Erin, too. They need anyone who can help and of course Dad and Erin are going to be there at the same time, helping. He's just not home yet, that's all. Maybe he went out for coffee with Erin, to talk. It's not a crime.

I push open the door and a blast of heat hits us. "Sorry it's so stuffy," I say over my shoulder to Vanessa and her dad. "I'll be fast." Ralph runs to the door. I flip on the living room light and pet him, then turn to Vanessa. "Will you check his food bowl?" Mostly that's to keep her from following me to my room, where I'm supposed to be getting this so-called item that I absolutely had to have tonight.

In my room, I take my school backpack out of the closet and look around for stuff to put in it: the gardening book I bought from the hardware store on Saturday — a lifetime ago. An extra pair of shorts. The rooster clock stares at me from my desk and suddenly I know just what to do with it. I put that in the backpack, too, which now looks nice and full. On the way out, I stop to pick up the picture of my mom and me that I keep on my dresser. It's from two years ago at my eighth-grade graduation. She's looking out from under her perfect ash-blond bob, her arm around me, smiling like crazy. She's beautiful. I got a citizenship award and a soccer award, and she was so proud of me, but it's Dad who's behind the camera, and really that smile is for him.

I take the picture. Instead of putting it in my backpack, I go into my parents' room and place it on my dad's nightstand, right in the spot where he usually sets his cell phone to charge while he sleeps.

Back out in the living room, I lift my backpack and say to Mr. Hathaway and Vanessa, "Got it."

Around three in the morning I wake up with the urge to pee. Quiet as I can, I slip the rooster clock out of my backpack, and on the way to the bathroom, I creep to Robby's door. It's open, spilling a faint yellow pool from his plug-in night light. I go in and set the clock, carefully, on his race car–shaped bureau.

Day 7

Friday

We leave for the prayer vigil at six thirty.

"You girls look lovely," Mrs. Hathaway says, smiling in a kind of sad way at us when we come out of Vanessa's room, ready to go. I borrowed a grass-green linen sheath dress from Vanessa, and twisted my hair up into a bun to keep it off my neck. Vanessa has on a blue and white flowered sundress; her short dark hair slicked back. We're dressed up like it's Easter Sunday or something, and I don't know if that's right, but we want to show respect.

"So do you, Mom," Vanessa says, and puts her arms around her mom. Her mom hugs her back, and in profile they look a lot alike with their short noses and short chins. I watch them and try not to think about how another whole day has passed without my own mom. Dad, at least, called me today. He wanted to check in and see how it was going, and I said fine, and he didn't ask if Mom called me back about brunch, and since he didn't ask I didn't say anything.

We go out to the driveway to get in the minivan, which Mr. Hathaway has cleaned out and kept running so that the interior is nice and cool. Vanessa and I take the second-row bucket seats; Robby is all the way on the back bench. I heard the rooster go off in his room this morning and he came running out in the hallway, and I went out there and teased him for a while about where it could have come from and how maybe it crawled in through his window and he should check to see if it laid eggs, then I told him it was from me. "Why?" he asked.

"Just because," I said, bending low so that I could look him in the eye. "You're almost eight. I got it when I was eight. An eight-year-old needs an alarm clock."

"Yeah," he said, nodding. "It does."

Mr. and Mrs. Hathaway are in now and we're all buckled up and ready to go. Mr. Hathaway looks back at us for a couple of seconds. "Everyone okay?" he asks.

"Yeah, Dad," Vanessa says.

Mrs. Hathaway doesn't turn. It's hard to tell for sure but she might be crying. The van pulls out and we drive the short distance in silence until Mr. Hathaway says, "Oh, sweet molly, look at all these cars."

The church parking lot already overflows into the street. There aren't any spots along the curb in front of or across from the church, either. A white KPXU van is double-parked, and so are two vans from the big network affiliates up in Dillon's Bluff.

"Drop us off here," Mrs. Hathaway says. "We'll save you a seat while you look for parking."

We pile out and head for the church, passing TV vans and camera setups that are taking footage of people going in. It's stinking hot, still. We've been inside all day; it was too hot even to go to Daniel's house for the pool. I have no idea how all these people are going to pack into our church and not die of suffocation.

One cameraman we pass has a blue ribbon tied to the handle of his canvas bag of gear. Mrs. Hathaway suddenly stops, staring at it. "Mom, come on," Vanessa says, "we need to get seats. Brandy Wilcox might be here."

"Maybe we'll get on TV!" Robby says, suddenly excited.

Then, Mrs. Hathaway whirls around, so fast that Vanessa and I step back. She grabs Robby's arm and looks back and forth between him and us. "Listen to me. This isn't a reality show. This isn't for being on TV, or for seeing a celebrity. If that's what you're here for, you can march right back to the car and tell your father to drive you home."

A few of the people walking by slow down. Robby's lip trembles. Vanessa pulls him close to her. "You don't have to yell," she mutters, red-faced.

"I'm sorry." Mrs. Hathaway's eyes fill. People walking by glance at us, curious. "But it could have been you, Vanessa." She looks at me. "Either one of you."

"We know, Mom. It scares us, too."

Then she takes them into a hug and I stand there in the hot parking lot, watching, until Mrs. Hathaway says, "Come on, Sammy, you, too," and holds us all tightly.

We find seats in a pew near the back of the sanctuary. It's crowded with people I don't know, people I don't even recognize. A lot of them have blue ribbons pinned to their shirts. A lady behind me tells someone else that she drove all the way from Wyoming with her daughter, who's fifteen. Like me. And I realize that this isn't mine, or Pineview's. Now everyone thinks they have a right to a piece of Jody being gone.

There was this boy in my eighth grade class, Ronnie Gomez, a scholarship kid. He died of leukemia halfway through the school year and suddenly all the kids were crying like they'd lost their best friend. People who had treated him like dirt before he got sick — because he came here straight from Mexico and barely spoke English, because he only had two outfits to wear to school — put up this memorial poster in the cafeteria. As if they'd ever even said hello to him, let alone visited him in the hospital the way I did, with my dad, touching the gray, sick skin of Ronnie's hand while we prayed by his bed.

"That's the way it is with most things in life, Sam," Dad said when I complained about the poster, and how no one even asked me if I wanted to sign it. "No one is there to see your finest moments and give you a medal. But that's not why you do good things, right?"

A Teachable Moment. A reminder about the parable of the workers in the field, how the workers just do what the workers do for the agreed-upon wage and shouldn't expect things to line up with human ideas of fairness. And then Dad ended up using it as a sermon illustration — changing the names to protect the innocent, and me.

Tonight, some part of me can't help but feel the way I did about Ronnie, and want all these people to leave. This happened to us, not them.

Pretty soon Mr. Hathaway, sweaty and out of breath, joins us. I can see the back of my dad's head in the front row. Jody's parents and Nick are next to him, with Erin and a few of the youth group kids in the pew right behind. There's still some sun coming in from outside, and also candles light the sanctuary, the way they do at Christmas. My dad gets up, and people start to quiet down other than a few whispers and rustlings as they try to make room for more arrivals.

Dad climbs the three stairs to the chancel. I know he's saying the Lord's Prayer under his breath because that's what he's done my whole life right before he speaks in church, to calm his nerves. I know there'll be a small Dixie cup of water on the shelf of the lectern. It used to be my special job to put it there, when I was little. I don't know who does it now.

He clears his throat.

"This will be simple and brief."

His eyes search the crowd. I sit up straighter so he can see me, if that's who he's looking for.

"Members of the Shaw family would like to say a few words. Then we'll hear from the choir, and have some moments of silence before heading out." He looks down at the lectern for a second, then up again, smiling slightly. "Don't worry — no sermon."

Titters of laughter.

"We're simply here to ask God to bring Jody home."

He steps away from the lectern, and Jody's mom and dad, and Nick, come up from their seats. I wonder how many people here are thinking about all of the rumors on the Internet as Jody's dad adjusts the microphone,

"Each one of you," he starts, then turns from the mic and clears his throat. "Each one of you," he says again, then stops and looks at Jody's mom and shakes his head.

In our pew, Mrs. Hathaway is crying very softly, and digging through her purse for a tissue.

Jody's mom steps up to the lectern to take over. "What Al is trying to say is thank you. For coming tonight, and for everything you've been doing for us and for Jody." I don't know how she's able to keep herself together, but she is, while Nick and Jody's dad look on with stunned expressions. "She's going to come back. We know she is. We believe in miracles."

How?

Jody's mom and dad go back to their seats while the choir files in and Gerald Ladew crosses the chancel, and I want to know *how* to believe in miracles. How *they* can, after all of this. How Job kept believing in everything. Does God give some people a kind of special faith? How does he decide who gets it? Or do you just decide that you do believe, no matter what, and then force your mind shut when doubts try to come in?

I used to think my faith was mine. When I was Robby's age, or even two years ago, I thought that what I believed was what *I* believed. Now I think maybe I'm just like Kacey Franklin, only here because my parents expect it. The difference is at least she's honest.

The choir is in place. Gerald approaches the organ with slow, deliberate steps, then suddenly turns and goes to the lectern where he stands in front of the microphone for a few seconds. We all wait, curious. He never says anything before the choir sings. One time he wrote an original piece for the choir and my dad asked him to introduce it, but Gerald said he likes the music to speak for itself.

He swipes a string of his thinning hair to the side of his head. "Jody," he says, then covers his face with one hand. He exhales a shuddery breath we can all hear through the sound system. Then he says again, "Jody. Has a beautiful voice. This is her favorite hymn. You can imagine her singing it."

I recognize the opening notes of an old hymn we haven't sung here in a long time, especially since we started having mostly guitar music during the service — after a big controversy during which everyone over the age of sixty threatened to leave the church if we didn't still have organ and choir every week, too. It's strange to me that this would be Jody's favorite. It's not "Amazing Grace" or one of the others that people always name. I don't think I even have a favorite hymn. I feel like I should.

"O Joy that seekest me through pain, I cannot close my heart to thee," the choir sings, sounding perfect, and a lot of people are sniffling and shaking now and I wonder how there could possibly be joy in this kind of pain. Vanessa is starting to cry, too, bent over with her face in her hands. But I don't feel anything. Just . . . numb. And suddenly I can't stand to sit here another three seconds in the stifling sanctuary with all these people who believe in this God, who's taken Jody, who's taken everything.

I get up, and try to stay bent low so that I'm not a distraction.

It's hard to get out. The church is thick with people standing in the back and they aren't quick to move out of my way. As I press my way through, I pass the small stained glass windows of Jesus's life, flickering kind of eerily in the candlelight. And I know it's the crowd and the heat and my imagination, but when I pass Lazarus I swear I feel his undead eyes on me.

Nick told me to find him after, so I wait. I stay half-hidden, sitting on the stone bench by the peace garden the youth group planted last spring on the side of the church. I can see people as they pour out the front doors but they can't really see me.

They come in waves — the strangers first, stopping to talk to the reporters that wait in the lot. Then the people who live here in Pineview but don't go to our church, like Cal from the hardware store, who pauses outside the doors and puts his hands in the pockets of his khaki pants, glancing around before descending the steps and going off to his car. Last to emerge are the members, lingering out front and hugging each other. The Hathaways come out and I can tell they're looking for me so I start to get up, but then I see Mr. and Mrs. Shaw, along with my dad, who's holding his hand out to the reporters that scurry toward them.

Next out is Erin. She's pretty, in a simple cotton dress that's kind of fifties style. I keep my eyes on her, trying to see if she's looking at my dad and if she is, what kind of look it might be.

Then I stop watching Erin because Nick comes out. He's with Dorrie Clark, and they're holding hands, and Dorrie's hair is beautifully strawberry blond and hanging over one eye in a way that makes her seem not like a teen girl but like a woman. I watch how she tucks a strand of it behind her ear and leans in close to Nick. I watch how he ducks his head to hear what she says. How he puts one arm around her protectively.

"There you are!" Vanessa sits next to me on the bench. I quickly take my eyes off Nick and Dorrie and anything in their vicinity. "Are you okay?"

"I think so. I just needed air."

"Your dad was looking for you."

"He was?" I stretch to see the church steps again, but the Shaws and my dad are gone now.

"Yeah, but then he kind of got mobbed by everyone, and we didn't know where you were, so . . ."

"It's okay," I say, standing up. "If he really wanted to find me, he could."

She spots her parents and waves to them. "My dad's going to bring the car around. Let's go."

KPXU
10:00 NEWS

It was a scene seldom witnessed in Pineview, hundreds of people — neighbors and strangers alike — united in hope at tonight's vigil for Jody Shaw, the local teen missing nearly a week. Despite six days of fruitless searching, the Shaw family has not given up hope that Jody will come home. Ex-

pressing her thanks to the community, Trish Shaw told the crowd that it's her faith that's keeping her strong during this difficult time. Frustrated investigators say that this is not the time to grow complacent, and urge the community to continue its vigilance. Here at KPXU we've had an unconfirmed report that several members of Jody's family, and two unidentified Pineview residents, have agreed to take polygraphs over the coming days. We'll keep you updated as we know more.

Troy? Any sign of this heat wave breaking?

Vanessa and I are in her room, in the dark. She's in her bed, and I'm on an air mattress, which is made of rubber, and even with two sheets it's making my back hot and sweaty.

I'm trying to not think about Nick and Dorrie by thinking about my dad, and how to get him to let me come home, but then I start to worry about Erin again and think of what I want to do with the yard instead — I need more rocks — then go back to thinking about Nick and Dorrie, and how perfect they looked together on the church steps.

"Are you awake?" Vanessa asks.

After a second, I say, "Yeah."

"I want to ask you something. And be honest."

"Okay."

"You know what Jody's mom said tonight? About how she knows Jody's still alive? Do *you* think she's still alive?"

I roll over; my rubber mattress squeaks. All the statistics say that Jody's probably not alive. Even after forty-eight hours, they said on the news that the chances go down to practically nothing.

And now it's been nearly a week. But I don't want to say, or believe, that Jody is dead.

"If it were you that disappeared," I say, "the way Jody did, just into thin air, it would be hard to believe . . . or accept . . . that you weren't alive, somewhere. Unless I saw for myself that you weren't."

"Like a body," Vanessa whispers.

"Yeah."

"Even if there was a *probability* that I wasn't?"

We're on the slippery edge of hopelessness, and I don't want to be the one to send us over. "I'd need proof. I'd need proof one way or the other."

"But there's a lot of stuff we believe in without proof."

I roll over again, onto my back, and stare into the dark.

"Not this."

Day 8

Saturday

At breakfast, Robby reminds Mrs. Hathaway about her promise to take him to the water park. "How could I forget," she says, transferring a pancake from the skillet onto Robby's plate. "Eat up and we'll get your stuff together. You girls sure you don't want to come?"

Vanessa holds up her fork. "The water park on a boiling hot Saturday, crawling with germy kids, including Robby and his two friends, who we'll probably get stuck with? Let me think." She pretends to consider before sinking her fork back into her pancakes. "Thank you but no."

"Great," her mom says cheerily. "That means you can weed the vegetable garden and check on the tomatoes and maybe run a vacuum through the house." She points her spatula at us. "And remember, don't go anywhere unless you get Daddy's permission. You stay here until he gets back from his golf game."

"Yes, we know," Vanessa says.

I've got my cell in the pocket of my pajama shorts while we eat, even though the Hathaways have a rule about no cell phones at the table. My mom has to get back to me today if we're going to have brunch tomorrow, and I don't want to miss her call. But by the time Vanessa's mom and Robby leave, there still hasn't been anything to miss.

After breakfast, we weed in our pajamas. We deadhead the flowers. We pick tomatoes and zucchini while Daisy walks up and down the rows, nose to the ground, getting in our way. And, we talk more about Jody's case, trying to guess who the unidentified Pineview residents mentioned on the news could be. "I bet it's people from church," Vanessa says. "Who does Jody even *know* other than people from school and people from church? I bet your dad knows exactly who's getting the lie detector test."

"I think it was a stranger who took her." I look at a tomato I've just picked and realize it's still hard, not really ready.

"Sam, every five seconds the news is saying how rare stranger abductions are. How it's like ninety-nine-point-nine percent likely that it's someone she knows. And if it's someone she knows, then it's someone *we* know. That's what creeps me out. How can I sit there at church knowing it could be someone over in the next pew?"

I don't know. "If it does turn out to be someone from church," I ask, "would you keep going?"

"Well, yeah." She looks at me. "After they caught him."

"I wouldn't." I step carefully through the garden and sit down in the shade.

She stops picking but stays where she is. "Why not? Whoever it is would be in jail."

"That's not the point."

"You'd be scared there's more people like that hanging around us?"

"No." Daisy comes over to me and I run my hand through her fur. "I don't know if I would believe in God anymore." If I do now.

She's still, and quiet, watching me. Then: "Your dad is always saying how there's evil all around us. Like, in us. That the scary things in life aren't the things out there . . ." She waves her hands around in the air. ". . . but the stuff in your own heart, and we all have it, so —"

"So, what?" I ask. "So that's supposed to make us feel better? That it doesn't matter if you go to church or not, or if you love your parents enough or not, or they love you and do their best? It's supposed to make us feel better that it's never enough? That no matter what, we're still . . . screwed?"

Daisy doesn't like the anger in my voice; she gets up and walks to the other side of the garden, closer to Vanessa.

"Isn't that the point of everything we believe?" she says. "That we need help?"

I don't feel like part of the "we" she's talking about, not right now. I used to be able to wrap my head around all of it, and I know that half the stuff she's saying is stuff I used to say to her when she was wondering aloud. This feeling that's been building, this doubt, since way before my mom's accident, has gotten bigger than me.

"I know we need help," I say. "What I don't know is why we're not getting it."

"Maybe it's like your dad says. We don't see how, or when —"

I interrupt her, unable to hear my dad's wisdom quoted one more time. "I *know* what he *says*, Vanessa." I get up and go inside, leaving her out there in the garden.

I take a shower, setting my phone on the back of the toilet in case anyone calls, but it doesn't make a peep. When I come out, dried off and dressed in shorts, T-shirt, and flip-flops, I can hear Vanessa vacuuming downstairs. I slip out and sit in the hammock to let my hair dry in the sun. A few dark clouds hang over the horizon like it might rain, or the clouds might do what they usually do: break up and disperse without giving us one drop. I call my dad's cell. It rings and rings and rings and finally goes to voice mail. When he got that phone he gave me this big speech about how he would have it on all the time when we weren't together, and I could call anytime, day or night, and no matter what he was doing he would absolutely, absolutely answer, if he possibly could. That was when I was in seventh grade and every day for a week my mom forgot to pick me up from school and I'd walk or get a ride with someone else and find her passed out in bed, dressed in her clothes like she *meant* to go out but got distracted.

And for a long time, Dad did always answer his phone. But not now. So he's either doing something that can't possibly be interrupted, or he's seeing my name flash on his screen and deciding, choosing, that I'm less important than whatever else is going on. The same way Mom has my message — my messages — and chooses not to call me.

"Dad," I say to his recorded voice, "can you call Mom about brunch? Maybe if she hears it from you it'll . . . mean more." Then I slide the phone shut and toss it in the hammock.

I don't care how much Vanessa's parents love me or how good a cook Mrs. Hathaway is. It's not home. I stand up, peek in the window — now Vanessa is vacuuming the upstairs with an irritated frown. Mr. Hathaway isn't home yet. The water park will take hours.

Vanessa's bike is parked against the porch rail, unlocked.

I tie my damp hair up into a knot.

I lift the bike down the steps and ride away.

*   *   *

It's been awhile since I rode a bike. Mine is collecting dust in our garage, alongside Mom's. But like they say, you never forget. It's not so easy with flip-flops on. I ride in a slow serpentine because I'm really not sure where I'm going. All I'd thought about was getting away.

I just keep moving forward.

Main Street is only a block away, and I think maybe I could go to the hardware store and look at more stuff for the yard, but I still don't have money and now I owe Cal.

It feels good to just ride. I don't know why I stopped. Well, I do know. I stopped because Mom stopped. We went through this biking phase, after Mom had a bad May. She was supposed to host a women's tea, in honor of the wife of a pastor in town who was retiring. Only she forgot until Vanessa's mom showed up in a flowered dress and a hat, with a plate of cucumber sandwiches. Mrs. Hathaway realized right away what was happening and took over so well that most people didn't even know anything was wrong. But Mom and Dad fought about it later. Mom said Dad should have reminded her. Then he said he did. Then she said he shouldn't have asked her to do it in the first place because he knew it was hard for her. And he said it's just a tea, it's just one afternoon, he thought she could handle it.

The next day Mom got me up early and we went to the Wal-Mart in Dillon's Bluff and bought bikes. "This is it," she told me. She'd put her hair back with a pink terry cloth headband and had on running pants and sneakers that were still nearly brand new from when she was going to take up running. "A new leaf."

When she handed the credit card to the cashier she told him about an article she'd read on how exercise could cure you of depression, make you sleep better, make you nicer, and give you good skin. I can't remember how many times we actually rode together. Maybe three.

But I didn't care if we were on bikes or organizing the house or watching TV or playing a game, as long as I knew she was okay. And now, I don't know if she's okay. Obviously at rehab she won't be drinking, but maybe she goes to sleep crying every night, or hates the people there, or the people there don't understand her like I do. Because I do. I'm the only person who knows what she goes through being Mrs. Reverend Charlie Taylor. Everyone expecting you to be camera-ready, all the time, like she said. Everyone expecting your husband to be available twenty-four hours a day for *their* supposed needs. And if your husband looks unironed or underfed or overfed or too pale or too tan or too rich or too poor or is late for something or forgets it altogether, it reflects on you.

Not that it's an excuse to drink. But maybe it is, a little bit? I don't know.

I think about the pamphlets from New Beginnings that are sitting in our house somewhere, unread, at least by me. Maybe I should take a look.

In the distance, thunder claps, and those dark clouds are coming in closer. It's going to rain; I can smell it. I pedal faster and realize I'm getting near the church, that somehow that's just where the bike pointed.

I ride around the block, twice. The lot is empty, which is a little odd since usually my dad and sometimes Gerald are here getting ready for Sunday. Even without going in, I know exactly how the sanctuary will look, how it will feel. I've walked up and down those aisles, between those pews, my whole life. It was home. And I guess what I feel now is that it's not. Like I've been betrayed, and — even though I know I could physically go in — locked out.

By the time I coast through the empty parking lot a third time and stop at the side entrance of the church, my shirt clings and my hair is coming loose from its knotted bun. The clouds are thick overhead. I lean the bike against the stone wall and stand outside the door. I know it won't be locked. Against the objections of the building committee, my dad always leaves this door — which goes straight into the sanctuary — unlocked, so that anyone who feels like they want to be inside of a church, any day, can.

There's a story in the Bible, a parable Jesus tells, about a widow who'd been done wrong. She shows up to the judge's house day after day, knocking on his door, demanding justice. And eventually, she gets it.

Even if some part of me feels locked out, I have a right to be here, a right to make my own demands.

I go inside.

It smells like wax. From the candles at last night's vigil. It's still warm, too, as if the heat from all those bodies hasn't had anywhere to go yet. Just one light is on — one of the chandeliers near the middle of the ceiling, and it casts just enough of a pale glow that I can see where I'm going. Not that I need it.

I sit at the end of a pew near the back, close to where I sat last night. Without the crowd here, I have a clear view of all the stained glass. Not just the big windows in the front but the side ones, too, the ones with scenes from the life of Jesus.

Rain starts to blow against the windows that are all around me, and every now and then a gust of wind rattles the door, and the sulfur smell of rain mixes with the warmth and wax, and I close my eyes and do what I haven't in a long time: picture myself there. There, with Jesus, in all of those places where he performed miracles, all of the places where he became who he was going to be. I imagine sitting on the bank of the river where he was baptized, and wonder if I'd notice the heavens opening up or if it was the kind of thing that was more subtle.

I imagine being passed a basket of bread that magically never gets empty, and taking a bite of the fish that feeds thousands. Would it be creepy, the way it never ran out, or would everyone just be laughing in that certain way you laugh when amazed?

I imagine being a shepherdess on the hillside when Jesus went out looking for his one lost sheep. Robes blowing around my legs. A rough wooden staff in my hands. The way it might feel to see a grown man coming back over the hill, carrying a lamb like a baby. It would make me love him, I think.

Mostly I picture myself crying outside the tomb of Lazarus, as one of his sisters, who as the story tells it were mad at Jesus because they'd asked him to come and asked him to come, and he got delayed, and Lazarus died. They buried him, mourned him. When Jesus finally got there, his sisters were like, what took you so long? It's too late. Lazarus is dead. And then Jesus tells Lazarus to come out, and he does, all wrapped up like a mummy in his grave clothes. But he wasn't a mummy; he was his real, alive self.

How would it feel to be so finally and completely dead, and then brought back to life? Did he know he was dead? His life afterward couldn't have been perfect. Maybe on bad days he'd get mad and wonder why Jesus saved him if it was just to have a hard, boring life like everyone else. Then maybe there were other days full of blue skies and fresh bread when he couldn't imagine missing out.

I mean, if it even really happened, which is the sentence I add now in my head whenever I think of any story in the Bible.

When I open my eyes, the tears spill out, and I ask anyone who might be listening, demand it: Let me believe again.

It's quiet for a long time. I don't know if I feel anything.

Then, a voice booms from behind me. "Samara!"

But it's not God, it's my dad. I turn around. He and Vanessa are standing there, wet from rain, both looking simultaneously relieved and angry. Vanessa more angry than anything. "Oh my God," she shouts, "why did you *do* that?"

I stand up. "I'm sorry."

"I mean what do you think I thought happened, Sam? You were there one second, then gone, and your phone was sitting there in the hammock like someone had just come and . . ."

"What's gotten into you, Sam?" Dad asks, coming closer, less mad than Vanessa, but still pretty mad.

"I borrowed your bike," I say to Vanessa.

"I know that *now*, because we saw it outside and that's how we knew you were here. But at the time all I saw was that you were gone."

"I'm sorry," I repeat.

Dad and Vanessa are soaked from wrestling her bike into the trunk of the car. Vanessa sits in the back with her earbuds in, staring out the window. Dad and I are up front. He's taking me back to the Hathaways'. When I protest, he looks at me in disbelief. "After all that, you think I'm going to leave you at home unsupervised?"

No, I want to say. I thought you'd supervise me.

When we get to Vanessa's, he tells me to stay put while he helps her get her bike out, because he wants to talk to me before I go in. She walks it up to her porch and waits. Dad gets back in the car and says, "We're going to talk about this tomorrow, after you've had some time to think."

"When tomorrow?"

"At brunch." He looks at me. "Mom called back. We're going to meet her at the Lodge."

Day 9

Sunday

Vanessa doesn't talk to me at breakfast. She tried last night, before bed, when she was helping me set up my sleeping bag downstairs on the sectional sofa. She didn't even want me sleeping in the same room as her.

". . . I'm just asking, Sam. Maybe you can't explain it to your dad because he's your dad, but you could explain it to me. You could at least *try*. To explain why you'd think it was anywhere near okay to just disappear, considering Jody."

"I can't explain" was all I could say to Vanessa. I almost called Nick about six different times during the night, but I don't know what I would have said to him, either, and anyway whatever connection I imagined I had with him was obviously just that — imagined. When he said to look for him after the vigil, that was just a polite way to end a phone conversation.

Now Vanessa crunches her cereal with a blank look on her face, staring past me. Mr. and Mrs. Hathaway aren't exactly chatty, either, mad that I'd put them in the position of feeling guilty or responsible if something happened to me. Even Robby seems like he's over the novelty of me living with them and keeps his eyes on the puzzle on the back of the cereal box.

I excuse myself from the table.

"We'll be leaving for church in ten minutes," Mrs. Hathaway says. "Meet us in the front room."

There's hardly anyone at youth group; just me and Vanessa and Paul and Kacey Franklin. Families are making their last summer trips before school starts, going on with their lives. I don't know where Daniel is. Erin hasn't planned anything for us to do other than sit around and talk about how we're dealing with the Jody situation, but it seems like no one is in the mood. Vanessa protests my stupidity of yesterday by keeping her arms crossed and refusing to say anything.

I'm staring at the COMMUNITY HAPPENS! poster wondering how it's going to feel to see my mom, when Kacey says, "Um, I guess I have something to share."

I look at her. We all do. I don't think Kacey's said anything in youth group, ever, except when we were discussing planning and organizing.

"Go ahead," Erin says, smiling encouragingly.

Kacey runs her fingers through the ends of her hair. "You know how I only come here because my parents make me? I could have stayed home today, with my brother, but I wanted to be here. I wanted to." When no one reacts, she looks around the room. "For real, that's big. I'm serious."

"What do you think changed?" Erin asks.

"I think I might believe in God." She says it almost with a shrug, like it's just that easy.

"Why?" I ask. Everyone stares at me, like I've said a bad word or something. Maybe it was the way I said it.

Kacey is the only one who takes my question seriously. "I think because of Jody."

134

The thing that has made me not believe in God, or not want to, or at least the thing that's pushed me over the edge after a year of doubt, is the same thing that makes Kacey believe?

"I don't get it," I say.

Vanessa unfolds her arms and sits forward. "She realized she needs help," she says to me.

"No," Kacey says, shaking her head. "That's not it. I think my parents make me come because they believe it's just what you do if you want a good life. Like, if you don't want bad things to happen to you. After Jody, it's like, now we all know that just because we come here every Sunday . . . that doesn't protect us from bad things happening, right?"

"Yeah?" Paul says.

I watch Kacey's face, waiting to see if I can grab hold of one little corner of her belief and let it carry me.

"But everyone's still here," Kacey says. "I mean, the vigil was packed. And I got here this morning and the parking lot's full. So all these people must be here for some other reason. Some real . . . *reason*." She looks around at us. "Right?"

"Right," Erin says, and we all stare at Kacey, like we'd never thought of that. Because maybe we hadn't.

After youth group, Erin pulls me aside and says, "So what's this thing about you running off yesterday and not telling anyone where you were going?"

I can't believe my dad, who barely has time to acknowledge that I exist, has somehow already managed to find a few minutes to tell Erin about yesterday.

"Come on, Sam." She smiles her open, clear smile, like I can trust her. "Let me help you figure it out. I'm good at this, it's my job."

I stare. "If you're so good at it, you don't need me to help you figure it out."

Dad, that I'm changing schools, or any other true facts about our lives. "Okay."

As soon as we pull into the parking lot, I see her. She's standing in the shade out in front, wearing a cotton skirt and sandals and an eyelet blouse. My breath catches. The parking lot gets blurry. I blink a few times and look at her again and think how pretty she is, and how small and thin and holding her body in this way that makes you think she's not sure something won't come along and blow her away.

She turns away from us and points her finger to the car and someone else comes out of the shade, a woman with short gray hair. I recognize her from the day we got our tour of New Beginnings. Margaret, I think, is her name.

Dad looks at himself in the visor mirror, touching his hair, while I watch Mom and Margaret talk. Mom shakes her head. Margaret puts one hand on each of Mom's shoulders and comes in close, like my soccer coach sometimes would, back when I still played, and she had to tell me something important about the game. Mom shakes her head some more. Margaret gets closer, bends her head as if to make sure Mom is really looking at her, really hearing her.

Mom is being coached. On how to get through lunch with her own family.

Dad flips the visor back up. "Okay. Remember what I said." Then he looks at me and blows air out, his cheeks puffing. "I'm nervous, too."

I nod, thinking we could be less nervous if we weren't trying to hide everything. That's been part of the problem all along.

When we get to where Mom and Margaret are waiting, I want to run up and hug her but suddenly I feel shy around my own mom, and she's frozen stiff, and I can't really see her face as it's hidden by her bob, which has grown some since she left and hangs over her eye. There's still a faint scratch and bump on her cheek from the accident. Then, she smiles a scared sort of smile and lifts her arms, and when we hug she holds on an extra second or two and says my name: "Samara. You look so beautiful." I inhale. Her hair smells different. She must have run out of her own shampoo. But she's still Mom.

I don't want to let go. When I finally do, Dad gives her a short hug and a kiss on the cheek but they don't look each other in the eye. His movements are jerky, and spots of sweat are spreading under his armpits.

Margaret folds her hands together and says, "Good, then." She looks at my mom. "I'll see you in an hour?"

Mom nods and I realize Margaret is her escort or chaperone, not just a ride. She walks toward the lot to do whatever it is she's going to do for the next hour while we have brunch.

"Do you want to sit out on the deck or inside?" Dad asks, still not quite letting his eyes stop anywhere near Mom's face.

"It's up to you," Mom says.

They're being so polite.

"Sam?" Dad asks.

"Either way."

He opens the door to go in. "I guess we'll just take whatever they've got."

Half an hour later I have my pancakes, Dad has his French toast special, and Mom has her two-egg breakfast, just like always, except now the tomato juice the waiter brings is just tomato juice. We did end up seated on the deck and at least half a dozen people from church have come to our table to say hi to my mom, tell her how great she looks, that they miss her, and ask how it's going. I wish this town had just one more place that was open on Sundays.

"Fine," she says.

"Thank you," she says.

And when they say they're looking forward to having her back, she smiles and says, "Me, too." But when another person asks when that will be, she says, "I'm not sure."

Dad glances up from his French toast. "Your thirty days will be up pretty soon."

She pushes some egg around on the plate, takes a bite of toast. Her eyes wander the deck. Maybe she's looking for Margaret to magically appear and tell her what to say to that. "Well."

That's all she's able to come up with on her own right away, but I have the feeling that if we wait, she'll say more. Except Dad suddenly changes the subject to Jody, talking about how the investigation seems to have hit another dead end. "I just wish they could figure out something," he says to his French toast. "Any little something to hold on to."

Mom should be irritated that Dad kind of hijacked the conversation, because that's something they used to fight about — how he's not so good at listening, how he doesn't notice when the things that are important to him aren't the same things that are important to her. But she almost seems to click on for the first time since we got here, and says, "I've been so sad about it. It's hard to be away while all this is happening, and watch it on the news instead of being a part of it. It feels at such a distance."

She could have returned my calls to tell me that. We could have been talking about Jody all this time. "I helped with the search," I say.

"Did you?" Mom gives me her full attention. And there's something about her eyes that tells me she's really here, truly, with us. Mentally, emotionally, physically *here*. I get a glimpse of some kind of reassurance that whatever she's doing and learning at rehab really is making her into her true self.

"Yeah, but then —" I'm about to tell her how I passed out and was sick with heat exhaustion and in bed for a day, all of it, but Dad interrupts me.

"Well, you've seen on the news how the search has gone," Dad says.

I guess I'm not supposed to upset her with the fact that I passed out. Pretty much every detail of my life right now is upsetting, so I decide that for the rest of brunch I'll only open my mouth to insert pancakes.

"I saw interviews with people coming out of the prayer vigil on the news," Mom says to Dad. "It sounds like it went well."

Dad agrees with an *mm*, and tells Mom a little bit about how many people came and what the choir sang and I stare out over the deck rail, into the foothills, into the woods, until the waiter clears our plates and Dad lays down the well-worn credit card and Mom blurts, "I'm thinking about staying at New Beginnings."

I turn my attention back to the table. "What?" I ask, even though I was afraid this is what's been coming.

"Beyond the thirty days."

"Oh," Dad says.

I flash on a picture of myself living in Vanessa's basement until graduation. From a school where I don't know anyone.

"I know we don't have the money. It's just that I think . . . I *know* . . . I'm not going to be ready." She folds and re-folds her napkin. "I feel like I'm just now —"

"How much longer?" I ask.

She sweeps her hair off her face and for a second I can see both her eyes. "I don't know. I need to talk to Margaret about it." Her hair slips back down. "You two are doing all right."

"No," I say.

Dad pats my arm. "It's okay."

Mom looks at me. "Aren't you?"

And from the feel of Dad's eyes on me, I won't be saying anything to Mom right now other than, "Yeah, we're fine."

Our credit card goes through — maybe miracles do happen — and we say good-bye to people on our way out, and Margaret is waiting at the hostess's desk. Mom hugs me good-bye. It's shorter this time because now I feel, I don't know, so disappointed and distracted. Dad kisses her cheek again. Back in the car, Dad lets out a big breath and I lean my seat back and close my eyes and wish I'd asked why she didn't call me back.

KPXU
LIVE @ FIVE

One week after the disappearance of thirteen-year-old Jody Shaw, presumed kidnapped, a national tabloid claims to know the identities of the men who submitted to polygraph tests on Saturday. *The National Investigator* reports that Donald Phillips, a teacher at Jody's junior high school, and Charlie Taylor, the pastor of Pineview Community Church, were both administered the test. Police Chief Marty Spencer would not confirm, and said that while they still do not have an identified suspect, they are building a profile of what this suspect may be like. They believe it is someone Jody knows and that this person is still in the area.

In the last week, police dispatchers have been swamped with close to 3,000 tips from around the country, including a Florida "clairvoyant" who says Jody is alive, possibly in Nevada. According to Chief Spencer, only about one tenth of the leads are worthy of follow-up.

The story of Jody's disappearance has now made headlines around the globe, moving the First Lady to place a call to Jody's parents, expressing sympathy and hope for the girl's safe return.

I'm staring at the TV, not sure I've heard right.

Mr. Hathaway mutes the news. Vanessa looks at me. "Did you know?"

I shake my head. Apparently my father did have a real reason for not answering his phone yesterday morning when I called. He was busy being a suspect. My face gets hot and my stomach hurts, but I don't want them all to see me lose it.

Robby, who's been lying on the floor on his stomach, watching, turns over and asks his dad, "What's a polygraph?"

"Lie detector test," I say. I crawl down onto the floor next to him. "The police have a *machine* that can tell if you're lying."

He looks worried, then asks, "Why did Pastor Charlie have to take a lie detector test?"

"Robber, bud, don't worry about it," Mr. Hathaway says. "He's just helping them find Jody."

"Oh."

"I'm gonna . . . ," I say, not bothering to finish the sentence as I get up and head for the basement.

"Sam?" Mrs. Hathaway calls after me. But what can she say? I just heard, along with the whole town, that my dad had to take a test to prove he didn't do something awful to Jody. I stop halfway down the stairs, realizing that Melinda Ford didn't say anything about the test results. Then my imagination goes wild and by the time I punch my dad's number into my cell, I'm picturing him in police custody, and all this is the real reason he sent me to live here.

He answers on the first ring. "Sam. I was just about to call you."

"Why didn't you tell me?"

"I didn't have a chance. I didn't know —"

"You didn't have a chance? We spent like an hour in the car together today."

"Honey, I didn't think it would get out. It was supposed to be confidential."

"Well, it isn't. Now everyone knows." I wonder if Mom saw the news report. And if she did, would that be the kind of thing that would make it hard for her to come home.

"Let me explain," Dad says. He sounds as urgent as I feel, and that makes me sit on the stair and listen. "The police asked everyone close to Jody's family to voluntarily eliminate themselves, just to give them some things to check off their list, no stone unturned."

"Why couldn't they *say* that on the news?"

"They don't like to tell the media very much if they think it could hurt the investigation. That's just how it works."

I wait for him to say it, but when he doesn't, I ask, "Well, did they? Eliminate you?"

He laughs in a big, relieved burst of breath. "Yes. Sam, yes."

"Dad. I want to come home."

He doesn't say anything.

I rephrase it. "I *need* to come home, Dad," and squint my eyes shut, afraid of his answer.

When he finally says, "Okay," I stand up and go straight to my duffel bag, ready to pack.

"Can you come get me right now?"

"Yes."

It's the first real yes I've had in a long time.

Day 10

Monday

My phone chimes with a text at two in the morning.

Are you awake?

It's from Nick. I stare at it awhile, baffled and still half-asleep. The house is so quiet, just the sound of the floor fan in my room and crickets outside the window, and Nick is awake a couple of miles away, maybe also hearing fans and crickets, and thinking of me.

I text back. *Sort of.*

Call me?

The hall, lit only by the bathroom night-light, is even quieter than my room. I find my flip-flops near the back door and slide them on before going into the garage through the inside door off the kitchen, where I figure I can talk without waking up my dad. After flipping on the light, I unfold a camping chair, sit down, and take a deep breath before calling Nick.

He answers halfway through the first ring. "Sam?"

"Hi."

"Hey. I didn't think you'd really be up."

He sounds like less than himself, and I don't think it's just because it's two AM. "Is everything okay?"

"I can't sleep, and really wanted to hear a friendly voice. And I thought of you."

Why me? I think. Of course that's not the kind of thing you ask.

"I saw you at the vigil," I say, "but there were so many people, and you looked busy with your family." And Dorrie.

"Oh, yeah. That whole thing was kind of . . . I mean, your dad did a great job with it and everything, but in a way it made me feel worse."

I'm so relieved I'm not the only one. "I know. I left halfway through to go outside. It was just hard. With all those strangers."

"That was part of it. Also, I don't know if it really makes a difference." He's quiet for a while then, before saying, "I don't mean I think prayer doesn't work. I'm just . . . Okay, you know when people at church say, 'I'll pray for you,' or something and you wonder if they really will? Like maybe they say it because it's what they're supposed to say in a church when you find out someone's life is gone into the crapper. Like, 'I just found out my mom has cancer and the doctors give her three weeks to live.' What can you say to that? So you say, 'I'll pray,' and then that person's mom dies in exactly three weeks anyway. Part of me couldn't help but think the vigil was that, times a million."

Nick mistakes my silence for something it isn't.

"Sorry," he says. "I shouldn't dump that on you. You probably —"

"No." Whatever he thinks I'm "probably" is going to be wrong. "I just didn't know anyone else . . . I mean anyone who's there every week of his own free will . . . felt that way. I think about that stuff a lot."

"Well, yeah," Nick says. "Everyone has doubts. But I didn't think *you* did."

"I do."

"It's good you've got your dad to talk about it with whenever you want."

"It's not like that," I say. "It's actually easier to talk to my mom about that stuff." There, my voice breaks, and I stop talking even though I want to add something about how that's why I miss her so much, why I need her now.

"Hey. She'll be back soon. It's going to get better."

And I don't know how he does that. How someone going through everything he's going through can say exactly what I need to hear, when my own dad, who does this for a living, can't. I nod, though I know he can't see me.

"Speaking of your dad, that's one reason I was thinking about you. I saw the news today. He talked to us about going in for the polygraph, so I knew, but after it got out I thought about how you'd feel, and I know how I'd feel. I mean I know how I *do* feel, with half the country saying it's me. And I wanted to give you advice, which is this: ignore everything everyone says."

"Okay. I'll try."

"Are you going to get in trouble for being on the phone this late? Or, I guess, this early?" He sounds better now than he did when this conversation started.

"I'm in the garage. My dad can't hear me."

"You're sitting in the garage at two in the morning. Now I really feel bad."

"I don't mind. I have a camp chair. It's comfy." I look around, noticing my bike hanging from a hook in the corner and my box of soccer trophies exactly where I put it last summer. "It is kind of hot in here, but my mom keeps it really clean. Kept it."

"I do that, too," Nick says. "I keep switching from present to past to present tense when I talk about Jody. Every time I accidentally say something in the past tense with my mom around, she gets this look on her face like she's hearing the news all over again. But when I say 'Jody is' or 'Jody does' or 'Jody likes,' that feels wrong, too."

I nod.

"Sam?"

"Still here. I was just thinking. About the past and present thing. And thinking at least I know where my mom is."

"But if she's not there, she's not there."

"Yeah."

"So," Nick says, "just how clean *is* your garage? Is it like OCD clean or regular clean?"

I laugh. "Well, it's a garage. Regular clean. A lot of stuff is in plastic storage boxes but not everything." I get up and walk to the big metal shelf where my mom keeps household stuff organized. "For example," I say, lifting the lid of one bin, "we have wrapping paper, ribbons, and cards neatly organized, but then there are some Christmas decorations sitting on top of all that because whoever put them away was too lazy to find the decoration bin. Probably me."

"That's good. You don't want to be too perfect."

"Some are labeled," I say, sliding out a large bin that's on the floor. "Like this one says 'winter clothes.' But I bet —" I pry off the lid. The bin is filled with bottles. Empty wine bottles, empty gin bottles. A few dozen of them, which must have been washed out carefully because there's only the faintest smell of alcohol wafting up.

"Winter clothes?" Nick asks. "Or . . . zombie remains? Though I guess the living dead can't really have remains . . ."

I put the lid back on. "Just . . . junk. Actually. Actually not junk. Empty wine bottles and stuff. My mom must have hidden them here so we wouldn't find them in the garbage."

Nick blows out a breath. "Man. I still can't picture your mom stumbling around drunk or anything. She always seemed — seems — so together."

"She is. She never stumbled around drunk like that. Most of the time we didn't even know. For her, even passing out was more like laying down to take a nap. It's not like it is on TV or anything." I want to change the subject. "Did you decide about college?"

He tells me about how he went online to pick out his classes, and talked to his assigned roommate on the phone. "I'm still not sure, though. They're holding my spot so I don't have to decide right this second or anything."

"I'm probably starting a new school, too. I haven't said anything to anyone about it yet."

"No more Amberton? Is that going to be okay?"

"It's too expensive. So it has to be okay. But . . . yeah. I'll still see Vanessa and Daniel all the time outside of school."

"You'll probably make other friends, too," he says, sounding so sure.

"Maybe." I can't see myself going up to someone at lunch and introducing myself. I yawn and try to catch myself in time to cover my mouth so Nick won't know, but he hears me and says, "I should let you get to bed."

"Probably."

"I'm glad you were up."

I don't tell him I wasn't actually up until his text woke me. "Me, too."

"Good night, Sam."

"Night, Nick."

After I hang up I sit in the garage awhile longer, going over our conversation, his voice. And what it means that he wanted to talk to me in the middle of the night. I don't know, maybe nothing. Maybe he's missing Jody. Maybe he's fighting with Dorrie again. Or maybe he truly likes me, just likes the person that I am. Maybe we're friends.

...

In the morning, I stay in bed a long time, listening to my dad get up, talk to Ralph, make coffee, shower. Eventually, he knocks on my door. "Sam?"

"Come in."

"Hey." Ralph trots past him and leaps onto my bed, purring and walking over my legs. "Not feeling so good?"

"Just tired. I guess I didn't sleep that great at Vanessa's." Plus there was my two AM phone conversation.

Dad sits in my desk chair. He looks tired, too, like he's acquired a few gray hairs and wrinkles he didn't have a week ago. "Why don't you come to the office with me today?"

"It's your day off." I'd thought maybe we could work in the yard together.

"I know, but I'm so behind with administrative business because of all of this with Jody. You could help Muriel organize the church library."

That's the part-time secretary who's worked at the church forever. "Muriel doesn't like me."

"Sure she does."

"Then she doesn't want help. Whenever I come to the office, she shoos me away and I end up with nothing to do but sit around and wait for you."

"I remember when you actually *liked* coming to work with me. You'd beg." He puts his elbow on my desk and leans his head on his fist. "What happened?"

I pet Ralph, who has settled on my chest, eyes closed to slits. It would take me all day to answer that question, all week. Dad doesn't have that kind of time. I try anyway. "Mom needed me."

He stares at me awhile. "When Mom comes back, I don't want

you to think that's your job anymore. Not that it ever was. I know that's kind of the pattern we got in. But it's not."

"Who's job is it, then?" I look at him, my hand still nestled in Ralph's fur.

"It's her job, Sam."

"But yesterday you wouldn't even let us tell her the truth. You *say* now it's not our job but you act like it is."

He rubs his face with the hand he's been leaning on. "I don't mean to. Yesterday, Sam, what can I say. I was very nervous."

Looking at him, I realize for the first time that it's possible he feels as lost as I do. Maybe what I've been thinking of as him being clueless is actually him not knowing what to do.

"Me, too."

For a second I think we're really going to talk. For a second I think this is the moment our whole relationship will change.

"Well," he says, getting up. "I've got to head out." He bends forward to give me a kiss. "Call me if you need me for anything. Promise?"

I nod, and watch him leave. What I said, about things changing because of Mom needing me, that's definitely at least partly true. But also, I grew up, is what happened. Why can't he see that?

Out in the yard, my plastic sheeting is in the heap where I left it, now speckled with dust and dirt. I start to pull it over the wild bushes and fallen-over hollyhocks but then stop halfway. I don't know what I'm doing. What if I kill off something that's actually not as already-nearly-dead as it looks? There are enough clouds in the sky to make me think we could get more rain today. Maybe I should leave all this alone and see if the rain helps. I sit down in a lawn chair and flip through the xeriscaping book, comparing the pictures of the plants in the book to what we've got. A lot of the stuff my mom and dad planted two summers ago matches up with what's in the book. They already picked some good drought-resistant plants; they just need maintenance.

I stare at the mess. It's too big a job for someone who doesn't even know where to start. Maybe I can get Vanessa and Daniel to help me with this later. If Vanessa will talk to me. Last night after my dad agreed that I could come home, I handed my cell phone to Vanessa's mom so he could let her know what was going on, and before he picked me up Vanessa watched me pack, sulking. "It sucks that much here, huh? You'd rather be home all by yourself?"

"It's not that," I said, shoving the last of my clothes into my duffel. "I just need one thing in my life to feel normal."

I think she could have understood if she'd tried, but I know that also she was still mad at me for taking off on Saturday. I'd be mad, too. Now, I get up and pull the sheeting over as much space as I can cover, and secure the edges of the plastic with rocks and the stone frog I gave my mom a few years ago.

My bike, in the garage, has a flat tire but otherwise looks okay to ride.

I pull the pump off the frame of my mom's bike and inflate my tire. I've got my phone, my key, and this time a ten dollar bill I took out of what I've been saving up for clothes. I open the garage and walk the bike out to test the tire. Technically, I'm still probably not supposed to go anywhere without permission, but Dad didn't say anything this morning and this will be quick. The tire seems to be holding its air. I close the garage and pedal away.

The sky is thick with clouds by the time I get to the hardware store. While I park the bike, I can see Cal through the window. He's sitting behind the register, reading a book. He looks up when I come in, bells jingling. His glasses are on the top of his head. "Hello," he says, and I can tell he's trying to remember my name.

"Hi," I say. "I have your two dollars. Thanks for the loan." I go to the counter and pull the ten out of my pocket.

"No problem." While Cal makes change, I ask him about container gardens.

"What happened to xeriscaping?"

"I'm still doing it. Only . . . my mom's been away, and I want to have something look nice when she comes back. The yard's going to take forever. I thought I could at least do one pot or box in the meantime."

He closes the register and puts his glasses on. "How long do you have?"

"I'm not sure." It could be a week, it could be another month. I err on the side of optimism, for a change. "Not that long."

"You'll probably have to go to a real gardening store and get some plants that have already started growing if you want it to really look nice."

"Oh." I'm about to ask him if he thinks it will work for me to transfer a cut of something from our own yard into the container, when the store rattles with a huge clap of thunder.

"Wow," he says.

I go to the storefront window and watch the rain start to come down.

"Is that your bike out there?" he asks. "You can't ride home in this."

"I'll wait a minute. Maybe it will stop." I don't want to call my dad for a ride and get in trouble again, even if he didn't actually say I couldn't go anywhere.

Cal comes around from behind the counter and stands next to me. Rain blows against the window; a few birds fly by, looking for shelter. "I thought your dad did a nice job with the special service on Friday," Cal says.

Thinking about my conversation with Nick last night about the vigil, I'm not sure what to say. "I guess."

"I noticed you ducking out early."

I look at him; he's looking at me, his hands clasped behind his back. "You did?"

"I think so," he says. "Green dress? I was way in the back."

"Yeah. I needed air." The rain hasn't slowed down at all, but I decide it's time to leave the store, which suddenly feels very empty. "Well, I guess I'll just deal with being wet. Thanks for the gardening tips."

"I could run you home, if you want," Cal says. "I don't think I'm going to get a rush of customers or anything."

"It's okay, thanks." My heart pounds but I try not to show it. He's just being nice. A ride home in the rain is the kind of thing anyone in Pineview would offer.

"You sure? I think it's going to be a pretty big one."

I shake my head. "It's okay. I'm not supposed to take rides, anyway."

He smiles and nods. "That's probably a good rule, these days."

Before I'm barely a quarter mile away, my tire is going flat again. I get off the bike and start to walk with it, against the wind, thinking about what just happened at the store. I hate this feeling of suspecting everyone, even the nicest people who are only trying to be good neighbors, but also I wonder if I should say something to someone. Not my dad, because I'll get in trouble for going out in the first place. The police? That feels extreme. I could call in an anonymous tip . . .

The rain finally starts to taper a little when Nick's silver truck comes around the corner, toward me.

He rolls down his window. "Hey! Stay right there."

The truck makes a three-point turn to maneuver next to me, and Nick jumps out. "Here." He picks up my bike and lifts it easily into the truck bed. "Get in."

"Good timing," I say, breathless, as I climb in.

"So, where are we going?" He revs the engine and glances over his shoulder before pulling back out onto the road. "Vegas? Paris?"

I rake my fingers through my soaked hair, hoping it looks okay. Water droplets make a trail down my back, inside my shirt. The rain has also left small marks on Nick's cargo shorts and settles in beads on the tops of his knees.

"Just home."

"I offer Paris and you take home? Fine." He looks over at me for a few long seconds while stopped at a crosswalk. "You okay?"

I nod. "Why?"

"I don't know. You seem a little upset."

"Just . . ." I shake my head. "The storm kind of snuck up on me." The farther away I am from the hardware store the surer I am that I was being paranoid.

"The rain is nice, though," Nick says. We drive a bit, watching it bounce off the hood. He glances at me. "Did you get back to sleep okay after we talked?"

"Yeah. Did you?"

"Sleep isn't really high on my list of achievements lately."

We're already almost to my house. It's like the first time Nick gave me a ride, which was only like five days ago, but this time it's different. This time it's like we're really friends, more equal. When

155

I think about how it felt to have his hand on mine, something in me hurts, but in a good way. And I don't want to go home. I just want to be with Nick a little bit longer.

"We could drive around some more, if you want," I say. "I mean if you don't have anything else you have to do right now."

"Nothing. I've got nothing to do." He immediately does a U-turn, letting the tires fishtail on the wet pavement. He grins. "Sorry. That's what they call in driver's ed an 'unsafe maneuver.'" He turns on the truck radio. "What kind of music do you like? I haven't even picked out my presets on this radio yet."

"Anything is fine."

"No, come on. I want to know." We're moving again, him steering with his knee, adjusting the wiper speed with one hand, fiddling with the radio with the other. "There's got to be something you like more than anything else."

"Country."

We stop at the last traffic light in town. Nick reaches for the radio again, and cocks his head at me with a little smile that I can't help smile back at. "Country?"

"Yeah. Country." I flick his fingers away from the dial, still smiling, almost forgetting for a minute about all the stuff that's wrong. I find one of the three country stations that come in from Dillon's Bluff. "Like this. Stuff you can sing along with."

"Let's hear it, then." The light turns green and Nick signals right. We're making a loop, staying within Pineview.

And he wants me to sing.

My throat seizes. "I don't really know this one," I say when I can talk. "Maybe the next one."

We ride along and listen to the rest of the song, Nick drumming his fingers on the steering wheel until, suddenly, he brakes, craning his neck to see something on the driver's side of the truck. I lean forward so that I can see, too. It's a giant poster of Jody. A small billboard, really, on the side of Murray's gym. With Jody's face and information about her height and weight and where she was last seen, a phone number, a website.

A car behind us honks. Nick doesn't move for a few seconds, then the car honks again, longer and louder this time, probably someone from out of town because people from here don't honk like that. Nick moves the truck forward, the windshield whipped by rain, which has gotten heavy again.

The song on the radio now is one I know, a ballad about lost love and regret that's been popular all year. I can sing every word. Nick rubs the heel of his hand into his eyes, driving slowly. I sing a few bars with the radio, my voice trembly and breathy, then I stop and turn it down.

"This is why I'm not in choir."

That makes him smile. I can make Nick Shaw smile, even so soon after him having to look at the building-size face of his missing sister. It's the happiest I've felt in a long time.

"You know what that reminds me of?" he asks. "You singing? You probably don't even remember this, but we danced at Heidi's wedding and you kind of sang under your breath while we danced."

He remembers dancing with me, just like I do. "I did? I mean, I remember us dancing but not me singing."

"I don't think you knew you were doing it. It was kind of funny."

"Kind of embarrassing, more like." I look out the window. We're getting close to my house again. "Can I ask you a question?"

"Go ahead."

"When you asked me to dance, at the wedding?"

"Yeah?"

I think hard about how to phrase this. "Did you do that because you felt bad for me, sitting there with nothing to do? Or did Vanessa or Erin or someone tell you that you should ask me?"

"Hmm . . ."

"Never mind," I say. "You don't have to tell me. You probably don't even remember."

"No, no, I'm just thinking. No one told me to or asked me to, I know that. Maybe I did feel a little sorry for you. Is that bad?"

We're at the last stop sign before my house. I touch my hair to see if it's getting dry. And to determine just how bad I look before I say what I'm going to say. "I guess not. I guess it's better than nothing. It's just . . ."

"It's just what?" He turns off the windshield wipers; the rain has slowed to almost nothing.

I feel his eyes on me. This won't be so hard, I think. He's got a girlfriend and is leaving for college soon and I really want to know. "Do you think guys could think of me as a real girl?"

He laughs. "As opposed to what?"

"As opposed to the pastor's kid. As opposed to shy and . . . whatever. Seriously." As opposed to a substitute little sister, I think. A placeholder for Jody. "Like when I go to a new school, how will they see me?"

We're stopped in front of my house, the truck idling. Nick rolls his window down a little to let in the fresh, clean air. He isn't laughing anymore. "You're totally a real girl," he says. "No doubt."

Then, even though he's been looking at me off and on this whole time, the way it feels changes, and we're both kind of staring at each other and all the sounds around us seem extra loud: the truck running, birds doing their post-rain singing, the radio still playing softly in the background. His eyes are intense. On me.

"Thanks," I make myself say, starting to open the door so I can get out before I die of embarrassment. "And thanks for the ride."

"Wait, wait." He holds my forearm for a second; the tingle goes all the way to my neck. He lets go and the intensity vanishes as quickly as it came. "I'm not just saying that. Look." He sounds like a big brother again as he pulls the passenger-side visor down, flips open the mirror. "Do you think your mom is pretty?"

"Yeah."

"She's beautiful, right?"

I nod. She is beautiful.

"Well you look like her." He points to the mirror, and I stare at myself. "Can't you see it?"

Maybe the eyes. Maybe the neck. I think my mouth is like my dad's, full and crooked lips. "A little," I say, flipping the mirror shut.

"Okay, then." And he smiles at me.

"Thanks again, for the ride and everything."

"No problem."

I get all the way to the front door of my house before Nick calls out, "Hang on!"

Breathless, I turn, ready for him to say, *You want to go get lunch?*

"Your bike." He gets out of the truck, lifts my bike out of the back, wheels it over.

"Oh, thanks."

Then he puts his arms around me for a quick, brotherly, youth-group hug. He smells like rain and dryer sheets. "Bye, Sam."

"Bye." I watch him climb back in. He waves to me as he backs out and drives away.

On the eve of the ninth day of the search for Jody Shaw, the Pineview teen missing since last Sunday, the volunteer command center at Library Square is dormant. The Shaw family and others coordinating the effort have decided to decentralize. At a press conference this morning, Al Shaw insisted the family is not scaling back the search; rather, they are focusing their resources on specific pockets of interest throughout the county, including the unincorporated woodlands and foothills that surround Dillon's Bluff and Lawrence Springs. Shaw and his wife, Trish, once again expressed their gratitude for all the cards and letters that have poured in from around the world.

Police Chief Marty Spencer said that his staff has been in the process of interviewing and eliminating suspects, and sorting through the tips that continue to come in. The voluntary polygraph tests administered over the past several days have not yielded tangible results. In the last week, 1,500 square miles have been searched, 150,000 flyers have been printed, and 37 horses, 19 trained dogs, 1 helicopter, and 2 kayakers have been used in the search. And yet, Jody Shaw is still missing and her abductor is still at large.

Dad comes home during the very end of the report, and stands behind me until Melinda Ford throws it to the weatherman.

160

"Everything go okay today?" he asks, putting his hands on my shoulders.

I turn off the TV and angle the floor fan with my foot, so it's blowing on me more directly. "Fine." All I've been doing since Nick dropped me off is sitting here thinking about him, that look he gave me, the crackle when he touched my arm.

Now it's Dad's chance to come through. With the TV off and only the two of us here, we can continue the conversation we almost started this morning. We can talk about Mom, when she's coming back, when he's going to stop going to the Shaws' every day. When we're going to face the fact that Jody is probably gone forever and try to adjust to our new normal.

"Hungry?" he asks me.

"Yeah. Kind of starving."

"Good. Erin's coming over with some food in about twenty minutes. I'm going to hop in the shower."

I turn around and stare at him. "Why?"

"Because it's been nearly a hundred degrees all day and I stink?"

"No. Why is Erin bringing us food again?"

"Funny thing about that. Turns out humans have to eat every day. Several times. Not very efficient, I know. Take it up with God." He leans his arms on the end of the sofa and gets serious. "And because she likes to cook, and she cares about us. I hope you can show her some appreciation."

I don't want her to care about us, I think. Not like this. How can he not see what Erin really wants? Or maybe he does.

"Okay, Sam?"

I nod.

*   *   *

Erin shows up laden with a casserole dish and, balanced on top of it, a green salad in a wooden bowl. "Can you grab the salad?" she asks.

I take it. Through the plastic wrap that's stretched over the top, I see the carefully halved cherry tomatoes and the expensive dark lettuce and the way the yellow bell pepper rings are arranged just so. Erin's hair is ironed shiny and flat. She has on lip gloss, and a white linen cap-sleeved blouse just low enough to show the dusting of freckles across her collarbones.

I want to close the door on her eager, smiling face.

"Um," she says, laughing, "can I come in?"

"Sorry." She walks past, leaving her trail of lemony brightness. "You can leave that on the counter," I say, following her to the kitchen. "Do I need to reheat it or anything?" I peek under the foil. Lasagna. My dad's favorite. There's no reason to make lasagna on a hot day unless you know someone loves it and you're trying to impress them.

"Oh, no, I got it." She takes a glass down from the cupboard and fills it with water from the tap, then leans against the counter and smiles at me again. Apparently she's staying. "Your dad said you've got a project going on in the yard. Can I see?"

"If you want."

I lead her through the sliding glass doors and point to the black plastic sheeting. "There's not really anything to see. That's all I've done so far."

"That's okay," she says, crouching down and lifting a corner the plastic. "What's your vision, here?"

"My vision?"

She stands up. "For how it's going to look after?"

"I'm not sure." I readjust the plastic where she lifted it. "Not so messy and wild, I guess. More like . . ." The rest of that sentence is *what they have at New Beginnings.* I don't want to talk about my mom, not with Erin. "Just not so messy."

"Sam," she says, "about yesterday, I'm sorry if I nosed in where I don't belong. It's sort of my job, you know."

"I know."

"I mean it's literally in my job description: 'Befriend and spiritually mentor the teenage participants in church life.'"

I nod. "Okay." Thinking: But it's not in your job description to be my dad's substitute wife.

"So if you want to talk to me about anything . . ." She looks toward the house. "I promise you it's confidential."

"I know," I say again, even though it's way too late for me to trust her now, with how she's made herself so pretty to come here and cooked my dad's favorite meal. I add, "Thanks," so that we can end this conversation.

The door slides open; my dad comes out, scrubbed and happy. "Maybe we should eat out here," he says. "It's marginally cooler than inside the house."

"No," I say, "let's eat in." Eating outside would feel too much like a celebration, a real summer night like real families have. "Mosquitoes."

After dinner, Erin wants to play Scrabble. I wait for my dad to say no, that it's late and we're tired, or that he has to go see the Shaws or make phone calls for work. Instead, he practically jumps up. "You're on. House rules say we can swap out blanks at any point during the game. I need to check my handheld for anything life or death, then I'll grab the board."

I clear the plates.

"I'll rinse," Erin says, standing.

Day 11

Tuesday

The air-conditioning suddenly starts working again. I wake up freezing cold and find my dad in the hall, staring at the thermostat. "Wow," he says. "That's weird."

I fold my arms and squint at it with him. "You didn't do anything?" I ask.

"Nope. It just kicked back into gear, I guess."

It's a miracle, I almost say, then change my mind. "It's too cold now." I go back to my room to pull on a hoodie. Dad follows me.

"I'll make you hot chocolate. Hot chocolate in the dead of summer. To celebrate our frozen house."

What does he think I am? Twelve? "Summer's practically over." I get back under the covers.

He stands there, arms hanging. All I want is him to say something to let me know he might have even a tiny inkling what I feel. All I want is for him to be as confident and right and real with me as he is when he stands up in the pulpit. Instead, he's mute.

So I ask, "Am I going back to Amberton Heights or not? I need to know one way or the other." I've already made the transition in my mind, but I just want him to come out and say it.

Dad sits on my bed, which means the answer is going to be long and complicated and not good. "The money's just not there. They give us tuition assistance, but it's not enough. And now with your mom . . . insurance covers some of that but not all."

"But what if she doesn't stay?" Ralph walks down the hall and past my door but doesn't come in. "What if Mom comes home next week when she's supposed to? Then could we pay tuition?"

He shakes his head. "We couldn't *really* pay it last year. An anonymous donor at church paid it."

"What?"

"Someone at church heard we needed help and helped." He tucks the sheet around my knees. "It's not the first time."

I kick out from the sheet. "Random people at church are always giving us money?"

"I wouldn't say 'always,' but, yeah, we get help."

"Why didn't you tell me?"

"You shouldn't have to worry about money." But I've been worrying about everything else — about Mom and about Dad and Erin, *and* about money, and he could let me in on at least two of those three things. I'm just figuring out how to put all that into the right words to say to him when he says, "I've got the pastor's fellowship meeting in Lawrence Springs this morning. I missed it last month, and I really should go. I know they'll all want to know what they can do to help the Shaws. The head of the board at Amberton Heights will be there; I'll see if there's any way we can get you in."

"Forget it," I say. "Don't beg."

"Expressing a real need isn't begging."

"Maybe you should express your real need to *our* church, for a raise."

"Everyone is having a hard time right now. Maybe next year." He gets up and looks at his watch. He's always getting up and

168

looking at his watch. Always on the way somewhere that isn't here. "You've got two options for today: come with me, or I can drop you at Vanessa's."

"Why can't I just stay here?" I want to call Nick, or stay here and think about him.

"You did that yesterday."

"That's okay."

"Not with me." And he smiles his I-know-you-don't-like-me-right-now-but-I'm-your-father smile. "So which is it?"

The choice is easy. "Vanessa's."

We go to Daniel's for the pool while Mrs. Hathaway takes Robby shopping for school clothes. Vanessa is a lot less mad at me than she was, but still not happy, and tells me as we unroll our towels on the pool deck, "I'm not asking any questions. If you want to tell me something, you have to tell me. Because I'm done asking."

I decided on the way to Vanessa's that I'm going to be easygoing today and not think about school or Jody or my mom or Erin or anything that will make me feel bad. I'm only going to think about Nick.

"Okay?" Vanessa asks.

I say, teasing, "That's a question."

"Ha, ha."

We watch Daniel do the backstroke across the pool, his pale flab showing above the blue water line. "I've never figured out how Daniel stays so white," I say.

"SPF 50."

It goes like that for a while, Vanessa and me laying out and Daniel getting in and out of the pool, us talking about nothing, joking around, being normal. And it's easy, somehow, to just choose to stop thinking about things that feel bad. I can choose to sit by

169

the pool and not think about the billboard of Jody, or the look on my mom's face when she said she didn't think she was ready to come home, not sit here and try to make myself believe in God, not worry about how I'm going to adjust to public school. Only a little more than a week after Jody being taken and the world changing forever, it's actually easy to let life go on.

I don't like it.

Life shouldn't just go on, not with everything that's wrong. How can we lounge around the pool? We should be doing something, anything, other than relaxing.

"Hey," I say. Daniel paddles over, Vanessa sits up. "I'm trying to fix up our yard before my mom comes home. Maybe you guys could help me."

"Sure," Daniel says.

I stand up. "We have ice cream sandwiches in our freezer."

"You want us to go *now*?" Vanessa asks.

"Well, yeah."

Daniel hoists himself out of the pool, his slick body landing awkwardly on the edge. "Let me dry off."

"I think we should wait until my mom comes back to get us," Vanessa says. "And ask her."

She'll say no, especially after how I ran off last time.

"We'll ask Daniel's mom." Daniel's mom is busy watching soap operas and will let us do whatever.

"Sam . . ." Vanessa is pleading.

Daniel stands there with his towel around his shoulders, like a cape. "What's the big deal?"

"The big deal," I say, "is that Vanessa doesn't want to get in trouble, or break rules, even though I know she breaks rules when she's with her other friends." Vanessa opens her mouth to protest. "No," I say, looking at both of them, "I know, like when you guys went to that party at the lake at the end of the school year. I know. You're only being this way because my dad is the pastor, and I'm me. You say I don't tell you things, but you don't tell me things. Only certain things. You're . . . Good Vanessa and Good Daniel when you're with me."

They're speechless for a few seconds, then Daniel says to Vanessa, "It's kind of true."

"But I *like* Good Vanessa," she says with a pout.

"We're just not supposed to go off alone," I say to her. "We won't be alone. There are three of us all together. It's close. We'll do some work in the yard, have ice cream, and come back before your mom even gets back from shopping."

She sighs. "Fine."

We all go in and change, then Daniel calls to his mom, "Mom we're going to Sam's for a little while okay thanks bye."

On the walk to my house I'm starting to feel a little bit hopeful. The temperature has dropped just enough that you can imagine a taste of fall in the air if you try. Nick Shaw thinks I'm beautiful. Daniel and Vanessa are going to help me make progress on the yard, and there is the air-conditioning miracle. Maybe going to a new school won't be so horrible. Kacey Franklin goes there. We could be friends. I can reinvent myself a little. Be less shy.

Then we round the corner. My dad's car is in the driveway. He's supposed to be forty-five minutes away in Lawrence Springs. My first instinct is to look around for Erin's car, maybe parked down the street, or maybe we already passed it and didn't notice.

"I thought your dad was gone," Vanessa says, recognizing his car.

"Maybe there was an emergency. With the Shaws or something." I slow down. "Maybe we should go back."

Daniel says, "We can't, because I have to pee. Seriously."

"He wouldn't really be mad, Sam. Like you said, we're all together and Dan's mom gave us permission." She pulls on my hand. "Come on."

It's just his car. There isn't any sign of Erin. This will be fine. I keep walking, and when I get to the door of my house, put the key in and make as much noise as possible. "Dad?" I call, tossing my keys loudly into the metal bowl near the door where we keep keys.

I look at the empty living room, and into the empty kitchen.

The house is completely quiet.

Then I see a purse on the kitchen counter. Erin's.

"Let's go," I say quietly to Vanessa and Daniel, who have followed me this far.

"What? Why?"

I push them toward the door. "Because."

"Let me just use the bathroom," Daniel pleads.

"No."

I finally get them all the way out the door, grab my keys, and close it softly. Vanessa and Daniel give me confused looks.

"There was a note," I say. "He's . . . sleeping. He got . . . food poisoning. It said don't bother him." I start to walk away from the house, fast, and realize they aren't following me. "Come *on*."

"I said I have to pee, no joke."

"You're a guy," Vanessa says, impatient. "You can pee in the gutter." She catches up to me. "Are you sure your dad's okay? Maybe you should have checked on him."

I don't answer, and break into a jog. I don't know where I'm going or where I want to go or who I want to see right now. But I can't tell this to Vanessa and Daniel because it affects them. It affects everyone. Stopping, I turn back around to face them. "You're right. I should go back."

"You want me to call my mom?" Vanessa asks. She looks worried for me, like she can tell there's something I'm not saying.

"No. It's fine. You guys go back to Daniel's. It's okay."

"Are you sure?"

"Yeah." I'm walking backward toward my house, making sure they keep going the other way. "Call you later."

I go around the side of the house, as if I'm going to go in the back door. Then I crouch down, and pull out my cell phone. With unsteady hands, I call Nick. He answers on the third ring. "Hey."

"Are you busy right now?" I try to keep the tears out of my voice but I can't.

"Sort of, but . . . are you okay?"

"Yeah. Never mind."

"No, wait, it's okay. What do you need?"

"Can you come get me? At the corner east of my house?"

"Um, sure, yeah."

I pull myself together enough to say, "I need you to take me to see my mom."

I wait for Nick at the corner, the whole time thinking: what if I'm wrong? I need to calm down, not jump to conclusions. There's no sign of Erin's car anywhere. Maybe she left her purse at our house last night. But then, I'm sure I remember her putting it over her shoulder before she left. Maybe she came to pick up the lasagna pan and left her purse. Maybe my dad's car broke down and Erin gave him a ride to the meeting. Maybe a lot of things. I didn't see or hear anyone in the house, I could just go back, walk in, and look around better this time.

But then Nick's truck comes into view and all I want is to be driving far, far away from Pineview and everyone in it. We don't have to go see my mom. We could just drive and drive.

Nick pulls over, and I climb in. The cab smells like fabric softener. "Hi," I say.

He smiles but mostly looks concerned. "Hey there." After I get buckled in, he asks, "So, what's the urgency level here? Am I driving ambulance speed, the posted speed limit, or normal Nick?"

"Normal Nick."

"And you know where this place is?"

"Yeah." I think I can remember the way. "Just head toward Dillon's Bluff."

As soon as we're on the highway, the rational part of me feels stupid, almost sure that there's got to be some explanation. I should call my dad right now and ask. But I'm afraid. And that makes me think about Cal yesterday in the hardware store, and how I hate thinking everyone is doing something wrong. Tears come to my eyes as I wonder if there's anyone in the world I can actually trust.

When Nick asks me, "What's the story?" I only say, "I just really, really need to see my mom," and that's enough for him.

We listen to country radio and make small talk and for the most part I'm able to keep calm, wiping away a tear now and then before Nick can notice.

When we pass a car dealership outside Dillon's Bluff, Nick looks at it longingly and says, "I want to get a shell for the truck. You know, something to put over the back? I could put an air mattress and a sleeping bag back there, and a cooler with some food and stuff. Then my truck would be like my own traveling apartment. I could go anywhere."

"That would be nice." I picture going with him.

"They're expensive, though. I can't ask my parents for any money right now. I'd have to save up. The problem is they don't want me to have a job during the semester."

"So you're going?" I ask. "For sure?"

"Almost for sure. My parents don't want me to put my life on hold."

Even the Shaws are starting to let life go on. How do you know when to do that? How do you know when to move on without exactly giving up?

We slow down behind a line of cars; up ahead there's a guy in an orange vest holding up a stop sign. Road construction. In the growing silence, I dare to ask Nick, "What do you think of Erin?"

"What do you mean, what do I think?"

"Just in general." The line of cars starts to inch forward. Nick puts the truck in low gear.

"She's a good youth group leader. A lot better than that dude we had two years ago. At least she doesn't force us to do skits and trust falls and all that crap. Why?"

I think about how to phrase what I really want to ask. "What do you think of her as, like, a girl? Or . . . woman, I guess."

"Oh."

"All the youth group guys have crushes on her, right?"

He shrugs. "Maybe at one time or another, yeah, probably."

"Did you?" I watch his profile, and know he'll be honest with me.

"I think I did when she first started. She's cute and energetic and everything in that outdoorsy kind of way. If you like that."

We're past the highway construction now, and moving at full speed, the cars separating. I roll my window down and stick my hand out to test the air. "It's cooler here."

"Higher elevation." He reaches to turn down the fan and rolls down his window, too, filling the car with the faint scent of the pines that grow thicker up here. "Why all the questions about Erin? Don't you like her?"

175

"I don't *not* like her." Or at least I didn't used to. "She brought us dinner. Twice."

"That's nice. That's totally Erin."

"She's a good cook."

"True."

"She'd make a good wife for someone."

Nick laughs. "Are you trying to set her up with someone or something?"

"No." I lean toward the window, letting the air blow on my face. "She just seems like she wants to be married. And guys like her. So why isn't she?"

"Don't ask me. Isn't she only like twenty-five?"

"Twenty-six." The truck crests a hill and the sign for our exit comes into view. "Seven more miles," I say.

We ride three or four of those miles in silence, then Nick asks, "Can I tell you something personal? No one knows, so you have to keep it secret."

"Okay." I put all the stuff about Erin and my dad out of my head so I can really listen.

"Dorrie broke up with me. She made me promise not to tell, and then when we both go away to separate colleges we're just going to kind of tell people we wanted to focus on school."

"Oh." I'm not sure if I should say I'm sorry, or what. "I saw you guys at the vigil. You looked really . . . together."

"Yeah, well." He glances at me. "When I called you? That was right after she texted me to say she couldn't handle it anymore."

It makes me see his phone call in a whole different light.

"Like, the media attention on my family is too much, it's all kind of depressing when she's supposed to be starting an exciting time of her life at college."

"That's . . ." I don't know how someone could break up with Nick. Especially with a text message.

"I don't blame her. I'd probably break up with me, too, if I were her." He doesn't seem too upset, but then, I don't know that much about guys and how they think. "I know it's hard to sit around with my devastated parents and a bunch of tragedy groupies, watching the news and dodging the media."

"Tragedy groupies?"

"Yeah, you know. People who suddenly turn up in your life when something goes wrong, because they want to say that they were there, and because their lives are boring until something shitty happens to someone else and they can have a piece of it." He has a little bit of a smile on his face, but also sounds angry in a way I've never heard before. "Anyway," he says, "you ready to see your mom?"

"I think the turn is up here," I say after we exit, and he slows at a turnoff onto an unpaved road. We bump over red dirt and rocks until we see the sign for New Beginnings. What looks like a big old farmhouse sits at the end of the road. "It's smaller than I remember from the day we brought her," I say as Nick pulls into the gravel lot.

He takes in the wraparound porch, and the pen full of goats grazing near the gardens. "This is rehab?"

"Yeah." Now that we're here I have no idea what I'm going to do, or say. I stare out the window. "How mad would you be right now if I changed my mind and wanted to go home?"

"Not mad at all."

"Let me think for a minute."

"No problem." Nick turns off the engine and we sit there and watch the goats, mostly brown and speckled plus one little baby black one. Through the open windows we can hear the sounds of cicadas and sparrows and cars going by on the highway.

"You should see the gardens," I say suddenly, opening the door to get out.

"Okay."

I lead him past the goats and around the side of the farmhouse. "That's the vegetable garden," I say, pointing, "where the residents grow their own food. It's like part of therapy. The brochure they gave us that first day says that healthy activity and being outdoors are important for them. And over here" — I walk him around to the other end — "this is the xeriscaping. Have you heard of that?"

"No."

"It's a special kind of gardening where you only plant stuff that doesn't need extra watering, stuff that can just live on whatever water is naturally there."

He surveys the garden. "Looks like a bunch of rocks."

"There's lavender, there. Juniper. Cactus."

"I see," he says, nodding. "Plus a bunch of rocks."

"Well, yeah." I let myself laugh a little bit. "The rocks help cover the soil and keep moisture in. I'm trying to do something like this in our yard at home so that when my mom comes back, it will be . . ." I stop and stare at the perfectly landscaped garden, and compare it to our yard, which is currently covered by an ugly black tarp. "Well, it won't be like this." But we can work on it together, I think, realizing that's what I really want. I don't want to do it alone, I don't want to do it with Vanessa and Daniel. I want to do it with Mom.

The back door of the farmhouse opens and a bunch of people come out, and the way everyone looks at us I feel like we've been caught stealing or something. Fortunately, Margaret is there and recognizes me. She comes over. "Sam? It's not a visiting day, I'm sorry."

I'd forgotten about the visiting days and non-visiting days. I'm partly relieved because I could just say, okay, thank you, bye, and be on my way back . . . where? Home? Where possibly my father is in the very act of . . . I don't know what?

"Can I see my mom for just a minute?"

The residents who have come out to work in the garden are all looking at me like I'm an imposter, someone who has violated their peace and quiet away from their families and anyone else who might actually need something from them.

Margaret relents. "I'll ask her. Come around the front and I'll let you into the waiting area."

She goes in through the back, and Nick and I walk around to the front, past the goats again, who glance up and are the only witnesses to the fact that Nick takes my hand for the last few steps up to the door, and then says, "It's going to be okay," before letting go. The crackle isn't as intense as it was in the truck yesterday, but it's there.

Margaret opens the door and leads us to the waiting area. Nick sits on a small sofa that has room enough for me, too, but I choose a wooden chair.

"I'll be right back," Margaret says.

When she's gone, I tell Nick, "I don't even know what I'm going to say to her. If she comes out."

"She will."

I keep my eyes on the coffee table, with its careful array of magazines and pamphlets and a box of tissues in the middle of it all. "There's this support group for families of the residents," I say. "But it's on Saturday mornings and my dad always has too much to do to get ready for Sunday."

Nick's not buying it. "That's kind of a crappy excuse."

Margaret comes back in alone. Nick stands, but I don't move. "She'll be out in a sec," Margaret says. "She wanted to fix her hair." A phone rings out in the hall. "Excuse me."

Nick comes over to me, kneels down, touches my knee. "You want me to stay? Or wait in the truck? Or what?"

179

I don't have time to answer, because my mom walks in. "Sammy? What are you doing here?"

She looks so good. Better than she did at brunch on Sunday, better than she's looked at home for a long time. I don't mean physically. Physically she's always pretty, put together. I mean now she's calm. Soft. Like she's comfortable here. And I know I can't tell her anything about my dad and Erin, not unless I know for sure and even then, maybe not. Not when she's just getting steady.

"Hey, Mrs. Taylor," Nick says, getting up. I stand, too.

"Hello, Nick. I'm so sorry about Jody."

And she comes over and hugs him.

She pats his back. She murmurs things that I can't hear. She's warm and dignified and beautiful in ways I'd forgotten she could be. When Nick pulls away he's got tears in his eyes.

Mom wasn't like this on Sunday with my dad there. I want her at home, and I want her at home like this, but now I don't know if she can be home and be like this at the same time.

Nick looks at me. "I'll be hanging with the goats."

When he's gone, Mom comes over and puts her arms around me and I'm already crying when I say, "I just wanted to say hi."

"Hi," she says, squeezing tight. Then she holds me out to inspect me, like we haven't seen each other in a year, like we didn't just see each other two days ago. She studies my face. "You look so grown-up."

I wipe tears away, feeling not so grown-up. More like a baby.

"Does your father know you're here?"

I shake my head. Her eyes shift to the door. "I didn't know you were such good friends with Nick Shaw."

"Only recently."

"Sit down." She sits on the sofa and pats it. I sit next to her. "I have a group meeting in a few minutes, and I have to go to it."

I picture her in a room full of other residents, talking about the things that make them want to drink, things like their families, maybe. "Do you like the meetings?" I ask.

"Sometimes."

"You like the people?"

"Some of them." She brushes a piece of hair out of my eyes. "Are you okay? Is everything all right?"

I nod, because if I talk I'll cry again, and I don't want her to be stressed by me and worry that if she comes home it's going to be like this, me crying and not being all right. I want to say, "I miss you," but those are the words that will make me cry hardest.

"Sammy," she says, "I know." And she pulls me close. "I know. I'm sorry. I'm sorry." She kisses my head. "I've put a real wrench in things. It's not fair. I know."

"Are you going to come home?" I ask, pulling away.

And she looks at me. And I know that the answer is no, or at least, not yet.

I turn away. She hands me a tissue from the box on the table. "Why not?"

"Because," she says slowly, carefully. "I still have a lot of work to do. And I still need support."

"We'll support you," I say. "Me and Dad."

She shakes her head. "Your dad's not ready, either."

I want to ask her what that means, assure her that at least *I'm* ready, I think, but Margaret leans into the room. "Time for group, Laura."

"I have to go," Mom says to me. "I know you're angry —"

"I'm not."

Then she laughs a little bit. "Well, you should be. I am. And I'm learning not to be afraid anymore of being angry. I want you to know it's okay for you, too. You don't always have to be pleasant and say yes and not do things that might upset others." She holds the box of tissues out to me. "That includes me."

I take one, and blow my nose, wanting to tell her again that I'm not angry with her. But maybe that's not totally true.

"And," she adds, because she knows me, "you're allowed to be angry with your father."

Somehow I'm not having a problem with that, I think.

"He's only human," she finishes. "We all are."

"I know."

Then she hugs me again, kisses me, promises she'll call later in the week. She says good-bye. She walks out.

"How was it?" Nick, sitting on the ground by the goat pen, looks up at me, shielding his eyes from the sun. One of the big billies ambles to the fence and sticks his nose between the wooden slats. I scratch his head.

"I don't know."

Nick gets up and stands beside me, propping a sandaled foot onto the fence. "How come you had to suddenly see her, anyway?"

I give the goat's head a couple more scratches and withdraw my hand. I'm thinking of the way my dad's shoulders sank last night when Erin said she couldn't stay for Scrabble. His car in the drive when he was supposed to be in another town. Her purse on the counter. My mom not being ready to come home. Us all being only human.

"I don't know," I say again, and turn back for the truck. "It was stupid."

"Let's get food. We can talk about it if you want, or not. Either way, I'm starving."

"Okay." We walk to the truck and I resist the temptation to look back at the farmhouse. In my imagination, my mom is standing on the porch, waving at me, wishing me luck.

Nick opens the passenger door for me and offers his hand as I climb in. "There's a cool little taco stand off the highway near here, I think," he says. "Is that okay?"

"Yeah. Good." I get my phone out of my pocket. The fact that Dad hasn't called or anything means he still hasn't realized I'm not with Vanessa and Daniel. He could still be in his meeting, or still be . . . I call him while Nick backs out, the tires crunching on gravel.

My dad answers. "Sam?" He sounds pretty much normal.

"Hi."

"Everything okay? You ready for me to come pick you up?"

"No," I say. So he doesn't know yet that I'm not where I'm supposed to be. And doesn't seem to know that I know that he was not where *he* was supposed to be, when he was supposed to be there. "Are you still in Lawrence Springs?" I ask.

"Just headed home."

"In your car?"

He laughs. "Yes. Who else's car would I be in?"

"I don't know." I look out the window. Nick and I are back out on the dirt road that led us to New Beginnings. "Maybe you got a ride with someone or carpooled to save gas."

"Not today."

My heart pounds. "What did they say when you asked about help for my tuition?"

Nick glances at me.

Dad pauses. "Well, no answers just yet. I put it out there, you know, and I'll follow up in a couple of days."

I fight hard not to let him hear the tears that I know are coming, as I give him one more chance to tell the truth. "You're on your way home now? From Lawrence Springs?"

Another pause. "Are you sure everything is all right, Sam?"

My stomach hurts, so much. "Fine. I'm at Vanessa's just watching a movie so you can come get me whenever you want." I slide my phone shut and turn it off.

"You're at Vanessa's watching a movie?" Nick asks.

I don't say anything.

We're on the highway now. My window is down, and the truck radio is off, so all we hear is the wind and the distant sound of sirens. Fire trucks headed to a brushfire, maybe, or police rushing to another semi rollover at that unexpected curve at the pass, or a motorcycle down and someone's body all over the road. More tragedy, more destruction.

Nick suddenly brakes and swerves down an unmarked road to our right. "Sorry," he says. "I think the taco stand is down here. It kind of snuck up on me. Or maybe I should just take you home?"

"No, I'm hungry." The big aching hollow in my stomach isn't hunger, but I don't want to go home.

We bump along, the road rough enough that I have to hold on to the plastic handle that hangs from the truck cab roof. Scrub brush and weeds and rocks line both sides of the road. It doesn't look like the kind of place where a taco stand could do any real business.

"Are you sure it's here?"

"Uh, no," Nick confesses. "It's been awhile. I think my memory is screwed up."

"Should we turn around?"

"Let me go a little farther. If it's not around the next bend or two we'll go back." We pass a bend. He takes another road. "Maybe this is it." Then another turn. "This looks familiar. Sort of."

There are no houses, no roads to anything that could *be* a house, no mile markers, no power lines. I wonder if the searchers

184

looked here for Jody, if this was part of the 1,500 square miles they searched, and how many other deserted stretches of scrub forest there are in the county and if those have been searched. She could be here. We could be driving by her, or her body, this very second.

And no one is looking for her. Everyone is doing what they do. How many people are sitting at home watching TV while Jody is missing, how many lounging in pools like I did today, choosing not to think, how many shopping, how many counting the money in their cash registers, how many giving a long kiss good-bye to the person who is not their spouse. All while God watches, if he exists.

And Jody, still, alone.

I rest my head on the warm metal of the truck door and at first just let the tears come out. The truck makes a lot of noise on the dirt road and I don't think Nick can hear me.

"Hey, Sam? I think we're lost. Really lost. And I have the feeling I'm going to be in trouble with your dad if he thinks you're at Vanessa's and really you're with me."

I lift my head and look at him, not caring that my face is probably splotchy and tear-streaked now. "It doesn't matter."

"Hey, don't worry, I'll get you home."

"I said it doesn't matter."

"Come on, Sam. Talk to me." He's driving slow now, and reaches over to touch my knee.

I look at him, and he's so kind, and so good. His whole family is like that. "It shouldn't have happened to you," I say. "It shouldn't have happened to Jody. She has so many people who love her."

He stops the truck. "It shouldn't happen to anyone."

And I stare out at the wilderness we're in, thinking about my family and the way we're islands, now, and if I could just drift my island away, they could go on into their separate lives and be happy.

And God, he could just let me go, too, once and for all, instead of this slow, endless betrayal.

"I wish it was me," I say.

"What?" Nick whispers it, sounding afraid.

"I wish it was me who disappeared." And my stomach lurches so hard I think I'm going to be sick. I whip off my seat belt and open the passenger door to jump out.

"Sam . . . hold up!" Nick grabs my arm and yanks up the brake. I jerk away and nearly fall out of the truck cab, and now I don't feel like I'm going to be sick but I run into the field of nothing, knee-length scrub scratching my legs, feeling the rocks through the soles of my flip-flops.

Nick's footfalls crunch behind me. "Sam, wait! What is it?"

But I don't know, I don't know what it is. Except I can't stop running, and I just want to lose myself in the desert, and either disappear forever or wake up from whatever this is. Everything that's happened since the day Jody disappeared seems like it's been part of some other reality, where I'm friends with Nick but fight with Vanessa, my mom in rehab is a better parent than my pastor father, and Erin and my dad do whatever they want and God doesn't care or do anything or stop it.

All the suffering, all the brokenness, and no one to fix it.

With 150,000 flyers and 37 horses and 19 trained dogs and 1 helicopter and 2 kayakers can't we at least, at the very least, find Jody?

"Jody!" I scream out her name.

Nick's footsteps stop for a second, then start up again, faster.

I keep running, calling Jody's name. Field sparrows rise up from the brush ahead of me.

"Stop it," Nick says from behind me, breathless. "Sam, stop!"

He catches up with me, grabs my wrist. We both fall onto a

clump of sagebrush and rocky ground. I'm on my stomach, Nick's body on top of mine. My hands bleed from trying to stop my fall.

"She's not here," Nick gasps into my hair. "She's not here, Sam."

He's so big, crushing me under his weight. And for the first time I know, can feel, that even though all the times I've been with Nick he's seemed more or less okay, all things considered, that he's as destroyed as any of us. Because he's crying now, too, big scary sobs against my neck.

"Nick," I try to say, but my face is in the sage. I can barely breathe. I need him to get off of me. I push my hands into the ground to create air space, but his weight keeps me down, so I turn my head to the side the best I can. "Nick," I say again. I take in as much breath as I can and say, as loud as I can, "I can't breathe."

It's like I'm not here. Invisible, inaudible, nonexistent while Nick cries and cries and smothers me. I put my hands on the ground again, and dig in my toes, and throw my weight back against him as hard as I can. It works well enough that I can wriggle out and roll over onto my back, gasping.

He stops, suddenly, and looks around and at me, blinking. "Oh, my God. Are you okay? Your face, your legs . . . you're bleeding."

"I know." Everything stings.

He crawls to me and, still half-lying on the ground, touches my scraped knee, scratched thighs, bleeding hands. "I hurt you."

I don't say anything, just take in air and try to think, think about this situation, being hurt and in the middle of nowhere with someone that really I don't know that well when you think about it, someone my dad has warned me about, someone who is, like my dad, maybe a suspect.

"I didn't mean it," he says. "I didn't mean to."

And suddenly I panic, hearing a double meaning in what he says, thinking about the sirens on the highway and how quickly he

187

turned off after we heard them. The way he grabbed my wrist so tightly, pulling me down, the way he said, "She's not here."

I stare him in the eye and whisper, "Where is she, Nick? If she's not here, where is she?"

A blank look crosses his face. Then a confused one. "What?" He scoots away from me and sits up. "No," he says. "No no. You don't think . . . Sam, no. No." He puts his face in his hands and starts crying again, quieter this time. "I can't believe you think that. I can't believe anyone thinks that." He lifts his face, takes one hand and rips up a clump of brush, throwing it into the empty field. "I wouldn't hurt her. And I wouldn't hurt you."

I want to believe, but I've believed a lot of things that didn't end up being true.

He crawls back over to me and looks me up and down, all my scratches and bloody spots. "This was an accident. I freaked out. When you jumped out like that, I thought you were having some kind of nervous breakdown or something."

I hear the sirens again, closer.

"Sam," he says. "I wouldn't. Do you believe me?"

Do I believe?

I believe just enough that Jody is alive that I think we should keep looking.

I believe just enough in my mom to try to make a garden for her to work on when she gets home.

I believe just enough in my dad that he'll have an explanation, even if that explanation is that he's only human.

I believe just enough in myself to know that even if I start in a new school I'll be okay.

I believe just enough in forgiveness that eventually we'll be a family again.

I believe just enough in God that I'm praying right now that Nick means what he says.

"Yes," I whisper.

Nick lies down next to me and puts one hand under my head, cradling it. He pushes back my hair, all undone and full of dirt. His eyes are red and puffy as he picks a few little bits of gravel off my forehead. "You're beautiful, Sam." His voice is soft.

He gets even closer, practically on top of me, and puts his other hand behind my head so that I couldn't move if I wanted to.

I don't close my eyes. I want to see it all: Nick's teary face over me, my hand resting on his upper arm.

His lips are soft on mine, and his hands on my head and neck are soft, too, not hands that could ever hurt me, I know it. Then, he stops, and rests his cheek against mine. I rub his back, touch his neck, his arms, his waist.

I want him to kiss me again and think that in a few seconds, he probably will, and we don't hear the cars pull up to the side of the road or the voices until someone shouts, "There they are!"

I watch from the passenger side of one police car, while Nick is in the county sheriff's. They've handcuffed him, because of "procedure," even though I've said over and over that he didn't do anything. But they saw me and my bloody scrapes, in the middle of nowhere underneath Nick, who they apparently told earlier in the investigation not to go over the county line. Just in case. Not until they knew more about what happened to Jody.

They ask me a bunch of questions about what we've done since the minute Nick picked me up. I want to start before that, with what made me call him in the first place, but they don't ask.

What I'll find out later is that Nick didn't tell his parents where he was going and didn't leave a note like he was supposed to, and something turned up that made everyone panic and there was a big news alert, and they came looking for him. A highway construction guy called the police saying he'd seen a truck matching the description of Nick's and that there was a young girl with him but all I know now is that they've called my dad and we're waiting for him.

"Nick didn't do anything," I repeat to the female officer in the car with me.

"We hope not."

When Dad shows up, he escorts me to his car, and we sit. He squeezes and unsqueezes the steering wheel, shaking his head. Sometimes angry, sometimes almost but not crying. "I told you that you couldn't be alone with him."

"No, you didn't."

"Yes. I did." He's silent for a few seconds. "You know you're not supposed to go off and do things we didn't plan and agree to."

I watch the back of Nick's head, what I can see of it, in the sheriff's car. I wish I could go over there and tell him it's okay, we'll sort it all out.

"Samara, I feel like you're not listening to me. I said you know you're not supposed to go off and do things we didn't plan and agree to."

"You were in Lawrence Springs. I didn't want to bother you. In your meeting."

He's quiet.

I add: "Nick didn't do anything."

Someone from the sheriff's department comes over to our car. He leans into the open window on my dad's side. "You all can go on home," he says. To my dad: "Did you tell her?"

"Tell me what?"

Dad won't look at me. The officer crouches down lower so he can see my face.

"Tell me what?" I ask again.

Dad closes his eyes, shakes his head.

The officer says, "They found remains."

Day 12

Wednesday

KPXU

SPECIAL REPORT

This is Melinda Ford, live at the search site just outside Dillon's Bluff, where hikers made a gruesome discovery yesterday morning. Here's what we know: three hikers were a few miles off the Ridgeline Trail when they literally stumbled onto a human hand, and immediately notified authorities. As you can imagine, there was concern that the remains were somehow related to thirteen-year-old Jody Shaw, who has been missing for nearly a week and a half.

Unfortunately, yesterday's confusion led to misinformation. A local radio station reported that Jody's body had been found, and that story was widely reported for much of the day. However, as of right now, it is not believed that the remains are at all related to the Jody Shaw case. The size of the hand and the state of decomposition led experts to believe that the hand belongs to an adult male deceased for at

least a month. There will be a press conference later today to confirm these details.

It's not all good news for the Shaw family. Sources tell us that Nick Shaw, Jody's eighteen-year-old brother, was taken into custody yesterday afternoon for reasons not made known and given a second polygraph. Neither the family nor the authorities have any comment at this time, but we expect that to be addressed at the press conference as well.

I'm in the yard, fiddling with the plastic sheeting and wondering how long it's going to take to thoroughly smother everything that's under there, though I guess I shouldn't worry about that since Mom's return is so . . . indefinite. I hear the back door slide open and look up; Dad stands there, watching, his coffee cup in hand.

"You need any help with that?"

"No."

You would think I'd feel happy and relieved now that we know that the remains aren't Jody's. In a way it feels like we should start the search all over again, like we've been given a second chance. But in another way, the more time goes by, the harder it is to not know anything, to just be in the dark. Knowing for sure, even bad news, would at least be one thing that's certain.

Dad tried to sit me down last night and talk to me about what happened with Nick. He tried to get the point across that this is danger, real danger, and I can't go on acting like everything and everyone is safe.

"I don't think that," I said. If anything I feel the opposite. Just because I trust one person doesn't mean I trust anyone else.

We went around and around, and eventually I wouldn't reply to anything and only sat there at the table with my arms folded, telling him over and over, "I'm tired."

Finally he gave up, and let me go to bed.

I didn't sleep. I stayed up nearly all night with my phone in my hand, on vibrate, hoping for a call or a text or anything from Nick. Over and over again I replayed being out in that field with him, the moment I knew I was safe with him and he was going to kiss me.

He didn't call. I worried that they'd put him in jail. I worried that all this is my fault, and it kind of is — he was just a friend giving me a ride.

I made one call in the night. To the police tip line, and all I said was, "You should talk to Cal at the hardware store."

The only call I got was this morning, from Vanessa. She started right in, sounding confused and hurt more than angry. "I didn't even know you and Nick were friends like that."

"How do you know what happened?" I asked.

"I heard my mom telling my dad. I didn't mean to but I was going to the bathroom in the middle of the night and they were talking in the kitchen and I kind of . . . stopped to listen."

"How did *they* know?"

"Your dad? The Internet? Who knows."

She asked me a bunch of questions and I answered with as little detail as I possibly could without making her hate me.

Now, Dad comes over and helps fix a corner of the sheeting that's blown up even though I told him I don't need help. "I made a couple of calls," he says, "following up on yesterday's meeting. Hopefully we'll hear something soon about tuition assistance. Lord, honey, your legs."

They look bad, but they don't hurt too much. It's my palms that still sting, and my elbow is sore from sort of landing on it when I fell. I take the sheeting from him. It might be easier to take his lies if they didn't roll off his tongue so easily.

"It's kind of getting too late, Dad. School starts next week."

"We'll hope for the best but plan for the worst, okay?"

I say nothing, and brush off my shorts, ready to go in.

Dad lowers himself into a lawn chair. "Sit with me here a minute, Sammy."

I shake my head, and keep my face turned away from him. He wants to talk about yesterday, I know, talk about Mom, talk about everything and then give me orders about how I should spend my time today, which will no doubt involve being dumped off at Vanessa's so he's free to do whatever it is he does.

As I pass him on the way inside, he gently takes my wrist. "Sit," he says, not meanly, but firm. I do.

"Tell me what the sudden urge to see your mom was about, honey."

For the last twenty-four hours, in my imagination, I've been confronting my dad about Erin. Asking him directly, accusing him, listing the evidence, demanding an explanation. Now that I have the chance, I can't. He's my dad. What I'd be asking is so personal. I'm not even sure I have the right to know, or if I want to know.

"I just had to," I say.

He takes in breath and opens his mouth, to say that's not an answer or to ask again, but something makes him change his mind and all he does is look down at his coffee. "I'm sorry if you think I've been overprotective. The world feels very different than it did, before."

"I know. For me, too."

"Everyone thinks I have answers about why this happened, but it's not like God has called me up on the special pastor's hotline and told me."

"Do you think she's dead?" I ask, and hold my breath as I watch him think.

What he wants to say is yes. Yes is all over his face. But he's a coward, and won't do it. The best he can do is, "I don't know."

I stand up and this time he lets me go in. Before I close the sliding door, I look back at him. "Dad?"

"Yeah, Sammy?"

"I don't want Erin to bring us dinner anymore."

The look on his face tells me everything that I thought I wanted to know.

I was right about Dad dumping me at Vanessa's. "It won't be for long," he says. "I just have to run to the office and to the Shaws' to help them prepare for the press conference, then I'll come right back for you."

"Whatever you want."

"If you want to come with me, you can." Neither of us have said anything else about Mom or Erin, but I feel like he's trying to prove to me that he's not going to do anything wrong, anymore, ever again.

"It's okay." I don't want to be in charge of him, monitor him, any more than I ever wanted to be monitoring Mom.

When I get to Vanessa's, Daniel is there, too. We hang out in the basement, watching TV and not talking much.

"Jeez, Sam, seriously," Daniel said when he first saw my legs.

"I'm fine."

Vanessa kept her eyes on the TV, where they have remained fixed for an hour now. When she goes upstairs to ask her mom about lunch, Daniel looks at me. "I'm supposed to be the buffer. How am I doing?"

"Great."

"So," he says, "what's your version?"

"Of why Vanessa is mad at me? Or of yesterday?"

"She's not mad at you. She just feels like she doesn't understand you anymore. That's what she told me, anyway."

I don't understand me anymore, either, I want to say. Or anyone. We all keep saying how different the world is since Jody disappeared, but even if she comes back it will still be different. For us, for her. Maybe she'll come home and her room will look unfamiliar, her parents will feel like strangers. Maybe she won't even recognize herself, the way I don't recognize myself, like I'm a stranger in my life and it's all going on around me and I don't know how to be, or who to be in it. I want to know where I am in this different world. Maybe I'm in the same place I always was, but I don't realize it because I don't recognize anything.

All I can tell Daniel is, "Nick didn't do anything. He gave me a ride to see my mom and that's all."

"And you look like you rolled down a hill of broken glass because . . . ?"

"That was my fault. The whole thing was my fault." I pick up the remote and change from the music channel we've been watching to a cartoon. "How's your calling coming along?"

"I don't know." He steals the remote from me and changes to a documentary about the history of pizza. "Now I'm thinking I'll go into sales," he jokes.

"Same thing."

Then he looks at me and says, "No, it's not. Don't say that. I didn't know you were so down on pastors and I kind of wish I hadn't told you."

It hurts me to know that. "I'm sorry. It's just different than you think."

"Well, let me find that out. Maybe you're wrong."

I nod. "Maybe."

Vanessa calls from the top of the stairs, "Grilled cheese or tuna?"

"Tuna," Daniel says, while I say, "Grilled cheese."

There's a pause, then Vanessa comes farther down. "Mom says she's not a short-order cook and you have to pick one."

"You decide," I tell Daniel, and go into the downstairs bathroom to call Nick.

It rings four times then goes to voice mail. "Hi," I say. "It's Sam. I just wanted to see how you're doing. So. Bye." I wait in the bathroom a few minutes in case he calls right back. He doesn't, and I fight the urge to call him again and leave another message, a longer one, with an apology.

Vanessa knocks on the door. "Sam? Did you fall in? Lunch is ready."

"Coming." I look in the mirror and study my face, searching for who I was, who I am, and who I might be after all this is over.

We're eating tuna sandwiches at the kitchen table — me, Daniel, Vanessa, Robby, and Mrs. Hathaway — when the report from the press conference comes on the radio. Mrs. Hathaway has it tuned to the oldies station because she doesn't want us obsessing over the news or scaring Robby, but right at the end of a Beatles song the DJ says:

"It looks like the best leads in the Jody Shaw case have gone no-where fast. Is it my imagination, or has this case been one giant screwup since day one? Anyway, the hand found on the Ridgeline Trail — definitely not a match for Jody. Also, Jody's brother Nick passed his second voluntary polygraph and after 'intense interrogation' the cops are saying he's not a suspect anymore. Oops, sorry, Nick! Hope we didn't permanently ruin your life! Our thoughts and prayers go

out to Jody and Nick and the whole Shaw family, and we hope that between the police and the FBI and the Sheriff's department and the media, somebody can figure this thing out. Meanwhile, if you're missing a hand, give us a call at the station. If you can find someone to dial the phone for you. Okay, back to the music here at 97.9 rockin' oldies . . ."

"Square one," Daniel says.

I look at Vanessa. "I told you Nick didn't do anything."

She nods. "You did."

Robby holds up one hand, staring at it. "Mom? How do you lose your hand?"

"Eat your lunch, Robby," Mrs. Hathaway says, turning off the radio.

At dinner time, back at home, I consider Erin's leftover lasagna then decide to make us a salad, which is one thing I know how to do. Dad and I eat in silence other than me saying, "I heard on the press conference Nick isn't a suspect anymore. I told you." And him replying, "I'm as happy as you are about that."

The phone rings while we're cleaning up. I answer; it's Mom. I think it's the first time she's called us since going into New Beginnings, and her voice is good, strong, like it was when I saw her yesterday.

"In case I didn't say it," she says, "thanks for coming to see me. It was so good to see your lovely self."

"You, too." I have no idea if she knows anything about what happened after Nick and I left her.

"Margaret reminded me yesterday that I need to practice saying what I feel . . . just saying it right out. I haven't been, and people in my life might be used to being forced to interpret everything and guess. I don't want you to have to guess whether or not I love you."

I nod, because suddenly I can't talk.

"Honey?"

"Yeah," I manage. "That makes sense."

"Oh, good. Sometimes I think Margaret is a nut case, shelling out crazy advice that can't possibly work. I'm trying to just trust her." She laughs. It's the second time in two days I've heard her laugh. Then she stops, and says, "I need to speak with Dad, if he's there."

"Okay. I love you, too, Mom."

I hold the phone out to Dad. He takes it, looking scared, and I go to my room to wait for him to come deliver the news, whatever it is, but after a long time he's still talking to her, in a low voice, and I can't make out the words. All of the possibilities run through my head, everything that could happen to our family. What I said yesterday to Nick, that I wished it was me and not Jody, I don't feel that now. I don't even know if I meant it, then, or where that came from. All I can say for sure is that, for a moment, that's what I truly felt. But something had called me back from that feeling, and it wasn't just Nick.

I lie on the bed while I wait for Dad, my mind drifting everywhere, until it lands on a prayer. I'm surprised, and resist it at first, but it keeps coming back. It's not words, so much, just my mind going blank and thoughts reaching up up up, me wishing I could climb through the ceiling and over the stars until I can find God, really *see* God, and know once and for all that everything I've believed my whole life is true, and real. Or, not even everything. Not even half. Just the part about someone or something bigger than us who doesn't lose track. I want to believe the stories, that there really is someone who would search the whole mountainside just to find that one lost thing that he loves, and bring it home.

And then, something happens.

These words move through me, but don't come from me. Not a voice. Not a burning bush or a dove from heaven. Just a sense, a hint, of . . . presence. Of me knowing it's going to be okay, and that I'm not alone. It fills my heart. And for a second I worry that I'm turning into one of those people who sees the Virgin Mary in a corn chip, or that all this has finally driven me completely crazy and I'm hearing voices. But then, why couldn't a face on a corn chip be true, anyway? We believe in a lot of unbelievable stuff. How can we pick and choose which miracles make sense and which don't? By definition, a miracle doesn't make sense.

It's a low hum. Like I'm not alone. It's comfort, it's words but not words, it's a song, it's warm hands around my heart. And even though Jody is gone and my mom isn't cured and my dad isn't here, even when he is . . . despite all that, I'm not scared. Whatever it is nestles down deep now, in a place where it can't be dislodged, along with everything that happened between me and Nick yesterday, belonging only to me.

Day 13

Thursday

Nick called me back last night, while I was waiting in my room for Dad to come in and talk to me after talking to Mom — he never did.

"Hey," Nick said, sounding tired.

"How are you?"

"Fine. I mean, you know."

"Yeah."

There was a very long and very awkward silence and it occurred to me that Nick might worry that I think we're boyfriend and girlfriend now or something.

"Sam," he said, but I cut him off before he could say more.

"It's okay, I know. It was a crazy day."

"I'm leaving for school." I figured he was trying to let me down gently, the unsaid "Therefore, there is no point in us really hanging out or anything" playing in my mind. Though that was sort of okay, too, after the moment I had, the prayer.

"Oh. That's good. Right?"

"My parents told me last night that I have to, basically. They don't want me to delay. Because if . . . if Jody never comes back then we'll regret it. That's what they said. Anyway," Nick continued, "I thought we could get together. So I can say good-bye. Maybe tomorrow? If your dad will let you out, and let you see me."

Nick, wanting to see me. And even though it's for good-bye, that means everything. "He will," I said. Maybe not willingly, but he won't really have a choice.

"I can come get you, like, eleven?"

"See you then."

So, this morning, by the time my dad gets up, I'm already at the breakfast counter having cereal, ready to build my case for getting to see Nick. He says good morning when he comes in, but nothing else, and makes his coffee then stands there with his coffee cup, staring out at the yard. After I rinse my bowl and put it in the dishwasher, I say, "Dad?"

"Hm?" He turns around, looking sad and distracted.

"I'm going to go out for coffee with Nick. He's picking me up at eleven."

"Sammy . . ."

"We're just going over to Main Street Coffee. He wants to say good-bye."

He looks at me for a long time. "Okay. Just be back by late afternoon. We're taking the Hathaways out to the Lodge for an early dinner, to thank them for having you."

"I will."

"Then we'll go up to see Mom." I can tell he's trying to sound upbeat, hopeful. "She invited us for a family counseling session."

"Oh. Okay."

"We have a few things to sort out before she comes home next week."

My heart speeds up. "She's coming home?"

He nods.

"Then what?" I step closer to him and see that his expression isn't just sad and distracted, but afraid.

"Then . . . we'll see."

On one of the inside walls of Main Street Coffee there's a mural of Pineview, painted by a community center art class a few years ago. I've been staring at it, over Nick's shoulder, because so far we haven't done a very good job of talking. It's me, not him. All I can think about is my mom coming home, and the "we'll see" part of whatever is about to happen. It's not worry that I'm feeling. I just wonder.

And maybe it's a little bit Nick, too. Ever since I got in the truck and he saw my legs and my elbow and the scratches still on my face, he's been acting a little rattled. He said, "Holy crap," under his breath, then, "I'm so sorry." I told him it was okay, I'm fine, but I think it's hard for him to see me right here in front of him like this.

Finally, I focus my eyes on Nick's face and say again, to make sure he understands, "It's okay."

He nods and looks at his iced coffee. I change the subject: "Are you all packed and everything?"

"Sort of. I think I need different stuff than I thought. It turned out my parents can't really afford the dorm double, so now I'm in a triple with different people . . . gotta work that out. One of them is from back east and a philosophy major. I forget where the other guy is from but I think he's studying psychology, like me."

"That'll be good."

He picks up a sugar packet from the ceramic bowl on the table, shakes it, then puts it back. "You know how I said yesterday that my parents want me to go so I'm not putting my life on hold, waiting for Jody? Well, also I think they want me gone." He looks at me, his coppery hair curling onto his forehead in a way that makes me want to reach over and touch it, push it back a little, the way a mother would.

"I doubt it."

"It'll take a long time for people to forget that for a couple of hours there I was the number one suspect in my own sister's . . . I mean, I think my folks think out of sight, out of mind is better for everyone."

I don't know what to say to that, because he's probably right in at least some small way. If this is good-bye, I don't want to say anything stupid and ruin forever the last time we talk. When I've let myself imagine us as a real couple — sitting together in church and holding hands and having dinner with each other's families and visiting him in college — I argue myself back out of it, trying to be realistic. I want to tell him not to worry that I have expectations. "Nick," I start, but he's already talking.

"You know it was just a week ago last night that you brought the brownies?" He shakes his head. "And now I feel, I don't know, closer to you than to anyone."

Then again, maybe I'm wrong about what's realistic.

"Me, too."

The guy from behind the coffee counter comes over to straighten the newspapers on a nearby table, and asks us if we want anything else, a scone or sandwich or piece of cake. "No," Nick says. "Thanks."

The employee leaves to help someone at one of the outside tables.

"I never really thought it was you," I say.

He shakes his head. "You should have. I mean, after the interrogation I got yesterday, *I* started to think for a minute it could be me. They laid out a good case. It messes with your head." He bumps his foot against mine, on purpose. "But thank you."

I bump back. "I'm sorry, though, for getting you in trouble."

"Don't be. When you called to ask me to come give you a ride to your mom's, I was so glad to have somewhere to go, and glad you asked me, and glad I got to see you."

I try, mentally and emotionally, to keep up with where this is going. To allow the growing feeling that mine and Nick's stories are not going to diverge, after all.

He smiles a little, and gets suddenly shy, staring intently at his coffee. "When I'm at school, could I write to you once in a while? Would you write back?"

My face is warm. I put my hands on my glass. "Yeah. I mean, I don't know if my dad is ever going to let me have my own e-mail address, but you can write me regular letters. You can call, too."

And then he looks up, and right at me, and the smile settles in his eyes that are reflecting me back to myself in a way I've never been seen before. I feel lightheaded when Nick says, "Maybe we should get cake after all."

I smile back, hoping my eyes are showing him who he is, too. "Okay."

Later, in the truck on the ride home, Nick gives me a refresher course on the gear shifting, and this time he doesn't let go of my hand until we pull up to my house. "Well," he says, sounding reluctant to be letting me go. "I'll see you soon."

"See you soon."

And he gives me a long hug and a short kiss and I manage not to cry until I see his truck disappear around the corner.

On our way to the Lodge, I roll down the window to let the air on my face. Pine trees whip by and a hawk soars and it feels good to be alive. With my head still half-hanging out the window, I ask my dad, "Does God ever talk to you?"

He doesn't answer, and at first I think he hasn't heard. I bring my head fully into the car. "Dad? Does God ever talk to you?"

"I'm thinking."

I roll up the window partway to cut down on the noise, and wait.

Finally, he says in his pastory voice, "I believe God talks to everyone, through the Bible and through —"

"No. I know all that. I'm asking does God ever *talk* to you. To *you.* Do you hear God's voice? Not in your ear, but inside you, somewhere?"

"I don't know, Sam. Sometimes I think so. But honestly, I don't know for sure." He half laughs, half sighs. "Right now is probably not a good time to ask, since I'm questioning every decision I've ever made since and including going into seminary."

I look at him to see if he's serious. "You can quit. Or take a break."

"And do what? I'm probably not employable in the real world." We pull into the parking lot of the Lodge. "Speaking of which, order something under ten dollars, okay?"

"Okay."

The hostess takes us to where Vanessa and her family are already waiting on the deck, and tells us if we keep our eyes peeled we might catch sight of some young moose that have been grazing the meadow between the Lodge and the foothills at dawn and dusk lately.

I sit by Vanessa. "Hey."

"Hi."

"Keep your eye out for critters, Robby," Mr. Hathaway says. "You'll be our official watchman."

Dad and Mr. and Mrs. Hathaway make small talk about work, and church, and a little bit about the Shaws, and how fast the summer has gone by. There's a feeling in the conversation like already we're putting this summer in the past, it's time to look forward. Mr. Hathaway asks me, "Ready for school to start up?"

"Yeah, except . . ." I look at Vanessa. "I'm not going back to Amberton Heights."

"What?" She lets her menu drop.

"Well," Dad says, "we're not totally sure about that. Something could change."

"Dad, nothing's going to change. It's okay."

He gives me a look that's a mix of surprise and relief, like he thought I was going to totally fall apart if Amberton didn't work out. But I'm not. I mean it, it will be hard at first but okay.

I say to Vanessa, "Maybe I'll be back later, but not this year."

"Thanks for telling me like one week before school starts."

"Vanessa, honey," Mrs. Hathaway says.

"Sorry," Vanessa mutters, picking her menu back up. "I just wish —"

"There's a moose!" Robby points excitedly to a beige dot coming out of the woods in the distance. Everyone at the table looks.

"I don't know, bud," Mr. Hathaway says, squinting. "I think it's your imagination."

We go back to our menus and Vanessa's eyes over the top of hers are apologetic, looking at me. "I just wish everything weren't changing."

"I know."

"What's the skinny on this assistant pastor deal?" Mr. Hathaway asks my dad. "Got a call from Roger Wilkins about that last night. Kind of out of the blue."

I look at my dad, curious.

"I can't work seventy hours a week anymore," he says. "The church can have me for forty, including Sunday mornings, no more. The money is in the budget. We should use it."

"Maybe it's not a moose," Robby says, "but it's moving." His small hands grip the back of his chair as he stares intently out at the meadow. I turn to see what he's looking at. The beige dot is more distinct now, not so much beige as a mix of colors that had been blending into the dry scrub behind it.

A mix of colors, including orange. An orange T-shirt.

I stand up and walk to the deck railing, my mouth suddenly parched. I wet my lips. "That's a person."

Blue shorts.

Red-brown hair. Like Nick's.

And the person comes closer. Others start to stand up from their tables, napkins dropping on the deck, and I can feel the realization of it ripple through the whole place like a wave, like an earthquake, until someone — a waiter, holding a coffeepot — says, "Is that . . . ?"

No one wants to say it, in case they're wrong and later on feel dumb and disappointed, like the hikers who'd found the hand. No one has the faith to say her name.

Except me, and I shout it. Shout it as loud as I can, and soon everyone is saying it, calling it out, frantically running down the wooden staircase that leads to the restaurant's herb garden, which has a gate that opens onto the meadow.

The person stops and looks behind her, as if for a second not sure if she should keep going or return to wherever it is she came from. Then, she breaks into a sort of limping jog toward us, all of us, running to meet her, a lot of us crying and saying things like:

"Slow down, you'll scare her!"

"Call 911!"

But all I can say is her name, over and over, thinking how I'll tell Nick about it later, and how he should be here to see.

"Jody!"

"Jody!"

"Jody!"

Day 14

Friday

KPXU

BREAKING NEWS

. . . To recap what we know so far: Jody Shaw has been found alive and relatively unhurt. In a scene that has the whole country talking, an astonished crowd at the Lodge restaurant just outside of Pineview witnessed the thirteen-year-old emerge from the woods where she'd been held at the cabin of forty-seven-year-old Gerald Ladew, a friend of the family and director of the Pineview Community Church choir, of which Jody was a member. Ladew's body was found shortly thereafter, dead of what appeared to be a self-inflicted gunshot wound. No note was found.

After being taken to the hospital for examination and observation, Jody was released to her family last night. The family has asked for privacy at this time, but spokesperson Charlie Taylor will be making a statement on their behalf later this afternoon.

Authorities say that Ladew was on a long list of possible suspects and was scheduled to be interviewed this week. We'll be back after the break to talk with Police Chief Marty Spencer about where the investigation went wrong, and how Ladew managed to slip under the radar for nearly two weeks — a question I'm sure we'll all be asking for months as the facts come to light.

But for today, an entire community celebrates a happy ending to this story, and the safe return of one of Pineview's own.

Day 16

Sunday

There are only a couple of us at youth group. The twins are visiting grandparents and Paul has strep and who knows where everyone else is — maybe sitting at home, glued to the TV. It's me and Daniel and Vanessa, and Allie. And Erin.

"So," Erin says, balancing her Bible on her knees after having just read one of the Psalms. "What a week."

"Um, yeah," Daniel says.

The energy in the room, around church, is strange. Everyone's happy about Jody, obviously, but bewildered about Gerald. Soon they'll be chattering about my mom and dad, too, making guesses about why the church has to hire an assistant pastor, and why my mom is home but not coming to church. That's one of the things we talked about in counseling. After everything on Friday we rescheduled for Saturday and it finally happened. Mom doesn't want to come to church. Not yet. She doesn't want to be "the pastor's wife." And then Dad said, well, maybe I shouldn't be "the pastor," and Mom said no, that's who you are, and Margaret said we should take all of that very slow.

Erin closes her Bible now and drops it on the empty couch cushion next to her. "I have to tell you guys something." She looks around the room with her earnest face, eyes landing for a second on each of us. "I'm . . . I got another job. I mean a different job. A really good one at a big church in Colorado. Pastor Charlie wrote me a recommendation and" — she glances at me — "I got it."

Vanessa cries out, "No! Why?" Daniel and Allie join in the protests.

"I'll be here a couple more weeks, then I'm going to move and start getting their fall programs in place." Erin brushes a tear off her face. "God is calling me to this other place and I want to go. It feels right."

"No, it doesn't," Daniel says. "It feels like crap."

Vanessa looks at me like I should say something but I stay quiet. It's not like I'm happy. It's sad. It didn't have to be this way, or turn out like this, but it did. And I'm the only other one in the room besides Erin who knows it's for the best.

"I'm sorry, you guys," Erin says. "I know it seems like I'm leaving *you*. But it's more like I'm going to *them*." She manages a smile. "Can you do me a favor? Can you guys pray for me?" Her eyes lock on to me. "Even if you kind of hate me right now?"

"We'll never hate you," Vanessa says. "I'll start. Sam can close. Okay, Sam?"

I nod. "Yeah."

One Week Later

I ride my bike to the hardware store. Big late-summer clouds roll across the sky, but I think I can beat the rain this time.

At the jingling bells, Cal looks up from the pile of coins he's counting and rolling. "Hi there," he says.

I don't know if the police ever talked to him, or if my anonymous tip came too late for that, or if he ever knew anyone called in with his name. All I know is I feel a little bit guilty for suspecting, and I'm glad it wasn't him.

Also, I need a job. I reach in my pocket and pull out the folded-up piece of paper and hand it to him.

"What's this?" He unfolds it, and sets his wire-rim glasses on top of his head.

"A job application."

"Oh. I didn't know I was hiring." He smiles at me and looks at the paper. "No experience. Very tempting."

"I'm trying to help out with the family finances. And it's pretty dusty around here . . . I could help you organize and keep things neat. Even a couple hours a week."

He nods, and refolds the piece of paper. "I'll run it by my business manager."

"Okay. Thanks."

On the way out I pass the rack of seed packets, and, on impulse, grab the one with the most colorful, huge, impossible-looking flowers on it. I turn to Cal. "How much are these?"

He puts his glasses back on and squints at the packet, then says, "How about I just deduct it from your first paycheck."

I almost ask him if he's sure, then decide not to overanalyze a good thing and slip the seeds into my shorts pocket. "Thanks."

The bells jingle behind me, and I pedal home.

One Month Later

Dad pushes the cart. Mom holds the list. Their backs are in front of me, together, their voices saying the most regular things:

"We could grill some chicken later in the week."

"There's a good deal on pasta sauce."

Mom's been home awhile now and we're adjusting. She has to keep reminding me and Dad that we don't have to walk on eggshells around her. And Dad has to keep assuring us that the change he's made to his work schedule is going to stick, he's committed. The church hasn't found an assistant pastor yet but he's sticking to his forty-hour-a-week schedule and turning off his cell phone for whole evenings at a time.

Mom turns to me now. "Sam, why don't you pick out some ice cream?"

I go down a few aisles to the frozen foods, stopping in front of the ice cream. The gourmet kind I like is on sale, but the store brand is, too, for less. We are about completely broke. Beans and rice, peanut butter and jelly, stretching our ground beef with oats, washing out every single plastic bag I use for my school lunches . . . broke. Our one splurge today is a new bag of potting soil for the single container Mom's been using to teach me xeriscaping. Even she has a goal of looking for a job after she's been home eight weeks solid. Margaret said not to rush things.

Of the cheap ice cream, two flavors are left: Rocky Road and mint chip. Dad isn't crazy about mint chip but none of us likes Rocky Road. I shiver from the cold air that wafts out of the freezer and let the door thunk shut.

I turn, moving the mint chip from hand to hand so I don't freeze my fingers. As I come around the corner where the eggs are displayed, I almost run right into Jody Shaw and her mother.

Time compresses. In one moment, I remember those thirteen days that changed me: what it felt like when I first heard she was missing, the heat on the day of the search, Nick's hand on mine in the truck. I remember standing on her porch with Erin and looking at the piles of flowers, wondering if the blue ribbons would ever come down. I think about the letter on my desk at home, the one I'm writing to Nick in response to his first letter to me, which came last week.

"Sam?" Mrs. Shaw is saying my name.

But I can't take my eyes off Jody. The Shaws haven't been back to church and Jody is doing home school for a while, so I haven't really gotten a good look. Jody's cut her hair into a little bob, no more braids. She seems taller, prettier. And there's something else. "You got your braces off," I blurt, as if that was the most remarkable thing that had happened to her all summer.

She smiles, showing straight and perfect teeth. She looks so much like Nick.

Mrs. Shaw starts moving their cart forward. "Tell your folks we say hello."

I step out of the way. My fingers are getting numb from the ice cream. Jody lifts her hand to wave good-bye. "See you, Sam."

I watch them round the corner out of my sight. I want to follow them through the whole store and watch them shop, watch them stand in line. I want to look at Jody again and study her. Her looking so different isn't just because she's growing up, or the haircut, or the braces. I don't know how to say it other than there were shadows there, in her face, in her mom's face. It makes me think of Lazarus. He must have had those shadows, too, after his miracle. You don't spend time in the tomb without it changing you, and everyone who was waiting for you to come out.

But I leave them alone, instead speeding up to find my parents, looking up and down every aisle until I find them. Dad is setting two cans of turkey chili into the cart while Mom studies the list.

"Here I am," I say.

They both look up at once. They both smile.

Acknowledgments

Thanks to Fred Burmester and Mark Miller for answering techni-
cal inquiries early on. Extreme gratitude to Tara Altebrando and
Ann Cannon for reading drafts. Kisses to Lauren, Sarah F., Sarah
M., Tara, Alan, John, Emily, Maggie, and Maryrose for always being there on the other end of the e-mail. Life without regular writing dates with Anne Bowen, James Dashner, and Emily Wing
Smith would be dull indeed. Hugs to Sarah Wick — I miss you
already. I love all you guys and gals.

Love and thanks also to Michael Bourret, for regularly keeping
me from going off the deep end, and for being a great friend and
first-rate partner.

Many thanks to the LBYR family: T. S. Ferguson, Amanda
Hong, Alison Impey, Zoe Luderitz, Ames O'Neill, Victoria Staple-
ton, and everyone who helps them. And thanks most of all to my
editor, Jennifer Hunt, who is nearly almost always right.

As always, bonus thanks to my husband, Gordon Hultberg, for
being here day in and day out in all of the unglamorous reality.

I'm thankful for Karin Bergquist and Linford Detweiler of Over
the Rhine for their generosity with beauty, and for their song "Idea
#21 (Not Too Late)," which helped me understand the questions I
ask along with Sam. I owe a debt of gratitude to them and to all my
other personal patron saints — the artists, musicians, writers,
poets, and thinkers who articulate pain without losing hope, and
whose boldness in doubt continues to show me the way.